I Am Without Love

Other Publications by the Author:

Jeremiah's God

I Am Without Love

❀

So I Search

Estella Slattery

iUniverse, Inc.
New York Lincoln Shanghai

I Am Without Love
So I Search

All Rights Reserved © 2004 by Estella Slattery

No part of this book may be reproduced or transmitted in any form or by any means, graphic, electronic, or mechanical, including photocopying, recording, taping, or by any information storage retrieval system, without the written permission of the publisher.

iUniverse, Inc.

For information address:
iUniverse, Inc.
2021 Pine Lake Road, Suite 100
Lincoln, NE 68512
www.iuniverse.com

ISBN: 0-595-31233-0

Printed in the United States of America

To Ethel

Contents

A Reconcilable Difference 1
babe 17
Mater Misericordiae 28
The Shrinks, A Love Story 39
The Delousers, They Who Know Where the Bananas Are 47
A Girl on a Bus 60
Crucify! 69
Emma's Lament 75
Liddy and Company 83
An Archetypal Critique 97
Will Kennicott of Main Street 106
Christopher Marlowe, A Renaissance Poet 111
A Study of The Idylls of the King 123

A Reconcilable Difference

Phyllis Stockton's red nails pinched the stem of the dead blossom, severing the drying stalk at an exact point, a sensible slash, room for new growth. Her fingers rummaged through the tough, green foliage to snap off any other dry leaves. Today she was using her right hand and could work quickly, much better than with her left, which never managed the clean cuts so important for a healthy plant. She alternated hands because of a household hint she had read some years before, a hint from a woman who had suffered a rash on her right hand until a friend suggested that she wear a glove when pruning her geraniums. Phyllis had found the glove cumbersome, so she cleverly alternated hands. She had never suffered the rash.

She returned the porcelain pots to the window sill, placing them at a precise angle to catch the sun's rays, making a picture-perfect scene, bright red flowers, snowy white curtains, and sparkling glass. She stared for a moment, then said, "Why do I keep them when I hate their smell so?"

Flowers in the trash, she returned to her kitchen only to be jarred by the ring of the telephone, jarred because her resolve, her daring with the flowers needed time to steady itself, to settle in, not be exposed to the ministrations of those who would plan this day, indeed plan her life. She could imagine her mother, rescued flower in hand, striding into her kitchen to insist, "You surely did not mean to throw these out!"

And it was her mother's voice, for real and unusually early, that invaded Phyllis' kitchen. She talked business, the transfer of some stocks, "It's silly not to, dear. You will get them some day anyway. What I have in mind is that if you will agree to do this I will have more cash income." She argued, "I did not go on that Senior trip to Alaska, fussing about money, and I know now that that was a mistake. I am getting old enough that if I am ever to do these things, I had better be about it!"

Phyllis misinterpreted her mother's message, "If you are short of money you should have told me. I don't want you doing without. Money for that trip could have been arranged easily."

"Phyllis, dear, that is not what I mean, not what I am trying to tell you! You're to have those shares now! Besides everything else, we could save some on inheritance taxes."

"Not that much, and I wish you would not talk about dying, Mother."

"I am not talking about dying! Don't be this way!" The tone of her voice softened, "Listen to me. I do not want you feeling guilty. This is my decision. I want to sell you those shares, now. Can you manage the cash? If not, perhaps you can transfer some of your utility stocks to me."

"Whatever. Call the broker. Call Lem."

A second decision for this day kept Phyllis by the phone, 'Should I call Alec's mother? She must be lonely, but she could take it wrong, think me bitter.'

"What about whacking the hell out of a golf ball?" Agnes Whitehill's voice, raucous even on the telephone, claimed Phyllis' attention. "A round before the party. Meg says it's marvelous therapy, hitting something, slamming something hard."

Phyllis always flinched when Agnes talked so rough, unladylike at best, but no one ever suggested reform to Agnes, now explaining, "If we go right away, we'll finish in time for the luncheon. By the way, we did get one of those back rooms, won't be noticed so much there, especially the drinking."

"Agnes. You promised."

"I know. But I may need an extra one or two myself today."

"I saw the obituary. I am so sorry, Ag."

Agnes refused the sympathy, "There will be no fake tears! What about the golf?"

"I can't." Phyllis shook her head at the telephone. She would not take on Meg this early, Meg loaded with quick fixes, glib from her talk shows, her 'groups', Meg spewing diagnoses every step of the way. "Go without me," Phyllis insisted to Ag, "I'll see you at the clubhouse." Then she lied, "I have things to do."

"Like what?"

"Well, if you must know, I have some telephone calls to make, and there's that stuff Alec left."

"Not today, Phyl. Stay away from his goddamned trash and stay away from the telephone! Didn't we tell you?"

"Yes, but…"

Agnes cut in, "Did his mother call?"

"No."

"Did she go with him?"

"Not with her hip the way it is, which makes me think she might be lonely."

"My God! I can't believe you! Let her be lonely! Or let him worry about her! Tell me, had she said anything about the fern stand?"

"No, nothing." Ag, proprietary, nosy and Phyllis hated it, but she said, gently, "Please, don't fuss about me, Ag. I'll see you at the luncheon."

"Phyl."

"Something else?"

"Please, not a word about that other."

"Of course not. I promise."

Agnes would remember the fern stand. How dumb to have hoped that it would be forgotten by everyone. A minor item, at least to Alec. His mother had given them the stand years before, carrying it, bringing it herself to their living room and lovingly removing the blanket and cotton packing.

"I know that you will take good care of it, and I hope that you enjoy it as much as I have."

The pedestal had looked silly and old-fashioned to Phyllis at the time, and she had resented the imposition of something second-hand in her smart new home. She was wrong as she had learned to love the stand and to appreciate its value, 'a ridiculous sum' if I remember. And Alec wanting to sell it. Thank goodness his mother stopped him, must be twenty years ago.

Reminded of Alec's poor judgment and his carelessness with what he considered to be unimportant, Phyllis went to the garage to examine the boxes and sacks of trash that he had left there. At the bottom of a box of discarded clothes she found a large manila folder stuffed with various business statements. Sifting through them, looking for an uncashed check or an unpaid bill she found statements from out of town hotels.

'Funny he didn't have these disposed of at the office, probably hiding it from his secretary, wasn't concerned about me. The idea, thinking I would divorce him on the word of some hired informer. Dear me, these really are not first-class places.'

A legal-sized envelope contained an obvious oversight, a memorandum about the purchase of a house. Phyllis was familiar with the address, recognized the location as that of a new real estate development.

'Out there? Really! Those places must run from five to six hundred thousand...he certainly does not have the money for that. She must do real well with that shop.'

Phyllis dumped the trash into plastic containers, then went into the house to return with a note that she attached to one bag, a note that instructed her handy man to deliver the bags to the address that she had found in the folder.

The telephone rang again, her broker, wanting to verify this latest change in her bank shares.

"Are you sure that this is a wise move, Phyllis? It puts a lot of responsibility on you. And remember our concern about the farm income this year."

"Mother insists, Lem. We'll go along with her."

Before dressing for her luncheon, Phyllis inspected the fern stand. The graceful heirloom stood before a large bay window, crowned by a magnificent fern that Phyllis herself had nurtured for nearly twenty years.

"Not a scratch on it. I do hope that that girl likes modern furniture, that she's one of those who hates antiques."

Phyllis had not wanted her own Merry Widow party, that gathering to dull the sting of divorce, but her friends insisted and she gave up trying to change their minds. You do not tell your closest friends that you dislike being around women who are drinking. Nor do you tell those same friends that you resent their questions, their prying, and their poking about in your private life. You do not say that to women who share their own problems and worries with you. Added to this, Phyllis had found some of the parties to be unpleasant affairs with cruel things said about the former husband who that day stood at some distant altar with a new bride on his arm.

Phyllis had started the parties, but her idea had been a get-together of close friends, a moral support thing for the newly divorced woman, a sort of tea-and-toast time. And her party had worked out well, as shortly after their divorce Agnes and Ed had decided that they did not want to live apart and they had remarried. Phyllis was proud of that.

The parties, however, became popular and spread beyond her bridge club. They now had a definite form with rules, rules that Phyllis labeled, 'frivolous'. As usual, no one agreed with her, with most of her friends insisting that the rules made the parties more fun, in Meg's words, 'more meaningful'. Loyalty was important to Phyllis, and she knew that she could be wrong in her own views, so she would comply with the rules today.

Phyllis was curious about divorce, more curious than hurt about her own divorce. She had not told this to anyone because she would not admit an embarrassment, could not talk about what she believed to be a deficiency in her own character. She did not miss Alec, did not miss him at all, and how does one explain that? Especially when you are puzzled by it yourself? When Phyllis thought about Alec living with another woman, she felt only concern that he was being cared for properly, listened to, his meals on time. 'Thank heaven we had no children'. I wonder if she…probably not, she is a career woman, probably one of those clever young ones…my concern is improper. Really!'

Phyllis had not cried about her divorce. Meg had sobbed for days and still broke into tears when reminded of the husband she had lost. Phyllis labeled that 'self-indulgent'. She did admit to being upset, perhaps outraged that Alec had broken his vows, had ignored that fact of agreements made, had set aside a code of behavior whereby one lived, made choices trusting that promises would be honored. Alec had betrayed all of that, had gone off with some young woman to go through all of the business of setting up housekeeping again, and him not that young.

"If he wants a new house," she had told Agnes, "why hasn't he said so? Instead of going off with a stranger?"

Agnes squashed a giggle, managed, timidly, "Would you prefer an affair? Some men do it that way."

"An affair? Alec? He's president of the bank!"

The trip her mother proposed was rejected just as emphatically. "If you are giving him this divorce, I think you should go to Paris, or on a cruise. Meet some interesting men, maybe a younger one. Get stirred up a little!"

"Mother! That's vulgar!"

"Oh, for God's sake, Phyllis!"

Phyllis rejected one rule. She put her watch in her purse. She had a meeting at five that had priority over a silly party. They could have a party without time, without an awareness of time, the time of the music beginning, the slow march to the altar, the time of a new marriage with the old one gone forever. Not for her. She was sensible, matter-of-fact. Let Alec get married, be in the fuss and flurry of what these young women like, bridesmaids, groomsmen all over the place, over-dressed, tasteless, not like her own wedding…'my dress, modest, expensive, but modest, long sleeved, my breasts appropriately covered, sacred songs, not popular junk, only white flowers in the church. Alec can have his childish affair, I won't miss that meeting.'

"I have come to dread these affairs," Phyllis confided to Eve Golding on their way to the country club. "We have become like those awful television shows, everybody talking too much, revealing too much, more show-off than help, I think."

Eve found this amusing, "Come on, Phyl, you know the parties are fun, and what have you got against television? I like the talk shows. Besides, what would Meg talk about if she didn't watch her—'resources'? That's what she calls them, isn't it?"

"Quit that. Quit being snotty. You know how good Meg really is, and what a time she's having."

Eve chuckled, "Of course."

"I'll admit I have watched some of those programs, but I cannot take them seriously, not even some of the ones on public TV." Phyllis lectured as she maneuvered the huge town car through traffic. "Furthermore, I think those talk shows are phony, set-ups, that people are paid to appear on them and say such outlandish, yes—don't be so smug, Eve—outlandish and sometimes even indecent things! And our parties are getting to be just like them."

Eve burst into laughter. "Indecent? Oh, Phyl, you are precious! You'll never change!"

Laughter like Eve's always puzzled Phyllis. She never understood the humor. When she would try to explain herself, her friends only laughed more.

Phyllis' party was a lavish affair, far more people than she had expected, many that she did not know, and worse, they were noisy, a noisy crowd of women with cocktails in their hands, talking and sampling hors d'oeuvres. The room was decorated with balloons, flowers, and some large garish posters, that Phyllis recognized as the work of an acknowledged lesbian, a new friend of Meg's. Phyllis was disturbed, particularly by the posters and by the fact that what she had agreed to, an intimate party with close friends, was in fact a loud affair with strangers, a loud affair that looked and sounded very much like a wedding reception.

"Who are all of these people?" She demanded of Meg, "They're strangers to me! I don't know half of them!"

"Don't worry, you will, Phyl old girl. You'll get to know them. They're friends of mine, friends that you'll get to know because you are now one of them!" Meg made a sweeping gesture with her hand, "Look at them. They're the ones you see scooting into places alone or in twos and threes, over-the-hill girls scooting in among the successful, at concerts, church, any place you go dressed up. They lunch together, ride together, and do charities together. They're the ones you didn't see when you were married! Married and so legitimate, so damned husbanded legitimate with your husbanded and legitimate friends! Come, I'll introduce you." Phyllis suspected that there had been more alcohol than golf in Meg's morning.

Dubbed 'our latest recruit to a new life style', Phyllis was led around the room to be hugged and patted and reassured. She hated it all. She felt more mauled than comforted, and she became tense from the strain of pretending pleasure while inwardly seething, 'Meg and Ag! What bullies!'

Meg was thorough, "And this is Jill. Wasn't it lovely of her to bring her poster for you?"

Phyllis gasped, Meg at her worst and with a woman that Phyllis would have discreetly avoided. She struggled for correctness, a civility, managed only a stiff, "Are all of these posters your work?"

"Yes. This is a new art form for me." Brushing her hand across a collage of pinks, the artist explained, "This is one of my latest. In fact it was inspired by your party."

For her own art purchases, Phyllis had always relied on the judgment of professionals, legitimate dealers. Now she looked at Jill's work, tried to find something that she could understand or feel, but she could not separate the art from the artist, and she stared helplessly at what she believe to be an expression of something sinful. Watching her, the artist guessed, "You are hating all of this aren't you?"

The implied intimacy upset Phyllis more and she barely heard the kind words that followed, "Don't be angry with this. Your friends don't know how else to help, and, oh yes, they do believe that you need help, that you need a place of loudness and craziness, a place of forgetfulness to get you through this day."

"No one knows how I…"

"Of course no one does." Jill hurried on, "But maybe it would help you to understand them, to know what they are trying to do if you read my poster. We are all in it. Look first at your friends, see their beauty, their grace, their lovely clothes, their exquisite taste. Then look at the poster. Notice that I have used no straight lines, just swoops of movement, upward strokes caressing the female form. I have tried to emphasize a spirituality, emphasize a higher beauty, the beauty of the world of the female."

"I don't know…it is so new to me…" Phyllis stepped back squinting at the poster and seeking escape. The word female always sounded coarse to her.

Agnes pulled at her arm, "Time to eat. Come on, Phyl, you're beside me at the head table."

Meg was mistress of ceremonies. She introduced Phyllis as 'The Merry Widow of the Day' and welcomed all to the party. She finished her introduction innocently asking, "If any of you has a good idea on how to make these get-togethers more meaningful or more fun, now is the time to speak up."

Immediately, a young woman called out, "I have a really good idea." Calls of 'Let's hear it' and 'Go Girl!' encouraged the woman and she stood, smiling brightly.

"I'm new here, and my name is Molly." She bravely faced Phyllis' guests. "Where I come from, we had a party like this, and someone knew of a game, one of those rainy-day things we played as kids." Her bright eyes searched the room for support. "The game goes like this, one person starts the story, using only one sentence, oh, and you're supposed to stand when your turn comes, stand up and start with giving your name, a sort of get-acquainted thing, too. Anyhow," she rushed on, "the first person says one sentence, and the next person adds a second. You are making up a story, and I suppose it sounds silly, but it really is fun, and if you want someone to start, I will."

Meg's "Oh, God, no" was drowned out by applause and the story started, a gruesome tale about the misadventures of a young athlete and several women who contributed to his sexual education.

Agnes growled, "Next time we'll bring in cheerleaders!"

Phyllis was too preoccupied with her own role in the day's program to take offense at the story. She struggled with, 'What am I going to say? What a mess!'

What does one say to a new wife? To the woman who has taken your place, and, Phyllis had learned, it makes no difference if she stole your husband or if you gave him away, society permits the exchange, even supports it. The twenty-six years that you devoted to creating and cherishing a marriage are cast aside, and are gone, are no longer available for a new life, and not available for a new love. Also gone are those that never identified and seldom captured the great goal that made youth so exciting. Gone is youth's sureness about the future. Bitter thoughts plagued the new widow, 'Should I publicly demand that she give me back hope, give me back a future, or, failing that, give me back my husband? Silly, just as silly as my worries about him, bad taste, inappropriate, and inappropriate the memory of this party. Drat their damned rules! Never again will I be part of one of these charades'!

Phyllis objected less to the first rule than to the second. The After-Dessert-Bash was a chance for an honest appraisal or a soul-searching opportunity for each woman to say aloud what she wished that she had said to her first lover.

At other parties she had said to her first lover. At other parties she had thwarted the intent of this rule by quoting a line from a book, some simplistic, easily ignored statement. No one had ever referred to hers as 'one of the good ones'.

The second rule defined the finale of the party. The guest of honor was to stand and reveal to her friends the advice she would give to the new bride. Some responses to this request had been funny, some sad, some memorable. They had ranged from "Thanks, kid!" to unsavory revelations about the groom. One woman had proven herself to be prophetic with, "Enjoy yourself, babe, until the next bimbo comes along, because come she will. I would say in about two years. Want to bet? Let's say two years, and let me tell you, Dearie, you've got a hellish second year ahead of you!"

Phyllis knew that she must not lie, must not be frivolous when her predecessors had been sincere. She could choose not to speak and had proposed this to Agnes whose reply had been direct, clean-cutting, "No one is persecuting you, Phyl, no one is trying to make you do something that is wrong for you, but what in God's name makes you tick? Are you so superior that you don't need sympathy, someone to listen to you?"

Phyllis' obvious hurt and shock did not stop Agnes, "You're a queer one, and, I think, a little unhealthy, wacko, to be honest! Wacko because you don't cry when you're hurt! I'll bet you haven't shed a tear over Alec! And you're freezing us out, your friends, friends who've been there! Come on, Phyllis, give!"

Phyllis' brooding was interrupted by sounds of an argument, Meg and Agnes, both of them more than a little intoxicated. Agnes had excused herself from the first round of the After-Dessert-Bash. "I gotta have some time to think this one out."

"Having trouble remembering the first time, Ag?"

"You forget, Meggie, we're the same age."

"Thinking about those guys in our high school? Having trouble sorting them out?"

"I'm sure you could help me."

Agnes had had 'another one' before her turn came the second time, and the alcohol plus her anger at Meg led to carelessness, "Well, let's see, what would I say to my first lover? Hmm, not that it's any of your business, but." She looked directly at Meg, then blurted, "I'm glad you're dead, you bastard!...How do you like that, Meg old girl?"

Phyllis was stunned, but Meg, also in an alcoholic glow, exceeded Ag's rashness. "Dead? Now, let's see, who's dead? Who that we know is dead?…Frankie Atwood? No, you never dated him, he was sick all of the time." Meg babbled on, the only woman in the room who was talking, "Let's see, who else? Maybe someone from out of town? A college guy? Somebody older? I'll bet that's it! Somebody older!"

Agnes stared at Meg, gradually comprehending the gravity of what she herself had done. Suddenly she rose, swayed a little, then grabbed a dinner fork and pointed it at Phyllis' face, "By God, Phyl, shut her up! Shut her up right now, or I swear to God I'll tear her tongue out with this fork! You promised, Phyl!" Agnes ran from the room, heading for the bar. Meg, abandoning her post, followed her.

'Leaving me to pick up the pieces, both of them,' Phyllis fumed to herself, 'Damn them, damn the pair of them, damn what they do to me, damn this thing, this salute to my so-called widowhood with its alcohol, its naughty posters, its…misery! A great start for a new life! Or, just more damage to an old one?'

But always disciplined, composed, Phyllis stood to address her guests. "I thank all of you for coming, for your support, and your good wishes. Now, I am expected to tell you what I would say to the young woman who tonight, so legitimately steps into my husband's bed. I would tell her that I believe that she has made a bad bargain, but I suspect that she knows this already. So, if you will excuse me, I must get Agnes home. Come, Eve."

Agnes sobbed all of the way home, huddled in the back seat, and held close to Eve Golding's ample breast. Edward was waiting for Agnes in the kitchen.

"No golf today, Ed?"

"No, Eve. I rather expected this, thought I had better be around."

Back in the car, now in the front seat, Eve demanded, "What was that all about? What is it that you and Ed didn't want me to hear?"

"Let it go, Eve."

"No! There is something terrible wrong with Agnes, and I want to know what! And don't take me home, we're going to your place. I want to talk!"

Eve hated the perfection of Phyllis' kitchen, so different from her own comfortable jungle. She sat waiting while Phyllis fussed at the counter with a plate of cookies, lace doily, no crumbs. 'She even stands neat,' thought Eve, 'so unbending, so correct, wonder if that's why Alec left her.'

Impatient, Eve challenged Phyllis' silence, "That was some party, your Merry Widow bash, Phyl, but I'll never go to another one."

"Nor I."

"It felt wrong from the beginning." Eve waited. No response. Then, "What is it with Ag, why so drunk, why so crazy? I want to know."

"Her father just died."

"Her father? I didn't know she had a father still living. Where'd he live?"

"Eve, please don't ask me about him. His obituary was in the morning paper. That's all I'll say."

"After that scene in their house? Come on, Phyllis, look at my blouse! This is Ag's makeup, Ag's tears! What's going on?"

"Eve, this is not my…" Phyllis stopped. After a moment's silence, apparently after making a decision, she explained, "Agnes has not seen him for years. He was institutionalized."

"Prison?"

"A place for the criminally insane."

"Criminally insane? What'd he…Phyllis! What are you saying to me? Phyl! Please God, no! What are you telling me…My God, Phyl! I can't believe—"

Rape. Incest, savagery, that close, that disguised. Eve shivered, a momentary spasm from an inner shock, a withdrawal, a hiding, a rejection of even the thought of such evil. She whispered, "How did you find out?"

"By accident. I walked into their house at the wrong time. I never go into a house without knocking first, but it was the time when she and Ed were having their troubles, those awful fights before the divorce."

Eve played with her cookie, broke it in half, then into quarters, pushed the crumbs into small piles, sorting out what she had learned, finding her own world suddenly less certain, less together, Phyllis' day stained, ugly. And Agnes. Agnes so hurt, so vulnerable. Eve reached for a scapegoat, something to flail at, somebody to punish. "Damn Meg and her rules! Her damned therapies! Insisting on dragging that gang to our party, that Jill and her awful posters! Did you buy one? I saw her trying to sell it to you."

"She wasn't trying to sell it, at least I don't think she was." Phyllis welcomed the diversion, "She's just one of Meg's new things. She was trying to explain the meaning of that pink thing to me, but I'm a lost cause."

"You saying that glob of paint had some meaning?"

"Yes. Something about the female world, about women being graceful, spiritual, insistent or something. I'm sorry, but when I watched those women today, I saw little that was insistent."

"Not even Fran Wilson's red wig?" Eve giggled.

Phyllis laughed, "She looked like Orphan Annie! A matronly Orphan Annie! Why'd she do it?"

"Bob put her up to it, wants to get a yellow one too!" Eve's laughter, the ripples of a rich contralto, filled the room.

Phyllis joined the game, "And how about Vera Hanson's face lift? She moved like a zombie, says she doesn't dare blink! Or turn her head!"

Eve, joyfully, "Tell you what, Phyl, let's go back, go back to the party room, some of them must still be there! Go back and put some truth into that poster. We'll draw Tod Hansen's roving eye right in the middle of it, then draw big red K's around that eye, big red K's for Fran's kemo. Let's go!"

"A ridiculous ending for a ridiculous party!"

Eve stopped laughing, "Ridiculous! Our party? What we tried to do for you, ridiculous?"

"I shouldn't have said that. I am sorry."

"But that's the way you feel?" Eve waited, then, "For God's sake, Phyllis, I'll never understand you!"

"I said that I was sorry."

"I wonder. You know, we tried to do something for you, tried to help you get through what must be hell on Earth for you, then you go around acting so damned superior! And damned cold! Like a zombie!"

Eve stood up, teacup in hand, "I want you to know that that party cost me a pretty penny, and a couple days of work. And for what? Something ridiculous!" Then sharply, "I'm going home. I'll walk!"

Phyllis watched as Eve rinsed the teacup, did away with the crumbs, saw her framed against the kitchen window, 'My window, yes, and my cup, my crumbs, even my garbage. Why couldn't she have just walked out?'

Drying her hands on a carefully pressed tea towel, Eve repented, "I'm sorry, Phyllis. I guess I am just upset, not thinking very well, but this is your second bomb today, and I still don't know what you meant by the first one. Why did you call Alec a bad bargain? For God's sake, Phyl, he's a man, not something you trade off like a car. You loved him once, you married him. Or, were you trying to be funny?"

"Alec is no joke, Eve. I said bad investment and that is what I meant. He was a bad investment of my life, and I think he will be for this girl."

"An investment? That's a weird way of talking about love. It's no wonder he left you…Oh, Phyl, I am sorry I said that."

"Don't apologize for what you believe, Eve. You and many more, I would guess." Suddenly, Phyllis felt released, surprising clarity, triggered by Eve's wavering loyalty. And by a tarnished gift, a sham, the hypocrisy of a party to celebrate failure and embarrassment. Now, a wondrous freedom, freedom to talk, to explore the real sham, "Alec broke an agreement, trashed and destroyed what little was left of our marriage, what I had settled for."

"Settled for? Settled! Come on—where are the words like love, feelings, sex?"

"I'd have liked all of that."

"But he turned to a younger woman. This has sex written all over it, or…did you shut him out?"

"That's too easy, Eve. Try again. We had sex, a duty thing. Remember? 'You have to put up with it, mother said, put up with the mess of it.'"

"You've lost me, unless…" Eve wished that she had left earlier. "This is really none of my business."

"Don't be shy. You were about to ask me if I am frigid. That's the latest, isn't it, the latest on the soap opera circuit? The latest trend issued for the talk shows? Or have you been talking to my husband's lawyer?"

"I don't want to hear this, Phyllis." Eve felt trapped, "I should have gone home. I'm leaving now."

"Wait. We've gone this far, and I won't have you believing a lie. I've got that much coming to me."

"Am I unable to love, the failure described by that same lawyer? I don't believe that, but how would I know?"

Eve waited, watched Phyllis as she folded and refolded a napkin, listened to her.

"After several years of disappointment, several years of frustration, I decided that I was just unlucky, unlucky to have married a man who could not see sex, could not bring to his marriage, sex as anything more than pleasure for himself. I settled for that, had to settle for that. Maybe this girl can change him. I never could."

"Why didn't you divorce him?"

"I considered it. Many times but really it was not an option. Things are so different now, from when it would have counted for me, the church thing, the scandal, the bank. People could make their disapproval felt. And Alec's mother was so opposed to divorce, so certain that it was a sin."

"What about your own mother? She seems liberal enough to me. Wouldn't she had supported you?"

"Hah! Mother is a late bloomer to the liberal cause, a very late bloomer!"

"But surely she'd have been sympathetic?"

"In her own peculiar way, yes, but she had boundaries, the 'right' people." Phyllis laughed. "Picture her scooping my brassiere into a dust pan, marching to the kitchen stove and dumping it into the flames. Not the 'right' boy, you see."

"What boy? Who?"

"Oh, just a kid. His father worked for the county. We were at a school mixer. He got me in a dark corner, mauled me pretty good. Ashamed, confused, of course I told mother about it."

"Were you hurt?"

"No, had a torn brassiere that she would not touch, disposed of the kid and the brassiere with a swoop of the broom and dust pan, brassiere tossed into the stove."

"Alec was a 'right' man, I guess I married him mostly to please my parents."

"Don't ask me why I did not look for professional help. I don't think it was there even if I had had the courage to try it. Another late bloomer. All I could have done was go to a minister or a lawyer. You know what they'd have said."

"Then, yes."

"I did read books, read them before any of you got into this new stuff. I found only a few, but I read every one, and I asked Alec to read them. He did not understand, would not understand, reminded me that I was well provided for—what irony! Me in a union with my father's bank!"

Eve reached for the joys, the rationale of her own life, "You've missed life, Phyllis! Missed everything! If only you could know what it is like for Larry and me!"

"You and Larry? Aren't you a little over the hill for that?"

"Over the hill?...Oh, Phyllis."

The new widow went to the meeting of the bank's board of directors. She went alone as her mother had begged off, "Without those shares, I am no longer a voting member."

Her broker was right. Bad loans and low farm prices indicated dividend losses. Phyllis tried to listen to the auditor's report, but she found the recitation of numbers to be boring and the intricacies of bookkeeping far more complicated than she thought necessary. Let those who like to play with numbers parade their skills.

The last item on the meeting's agenda was the yearly election of the acting manager of the bank, often referred to as the bank president. No one had mentioned the divorce, and the chairman of the board, who was conducting the meeting, had obviously decided that he would be most tactful if he said as little as possible, as quickly as possible.

"As you know," he began, "Our president, Mr. Alexander Stockton, is unable to be here this evening." Phyllis heard a few low rumbles of laughter, but the chair hurried on. "We all know what a splendid job he has done for us, that is, is doing for us, and I think a vote of acclamation for his reelection is in order." He cleared his throat…"I have taken it upon myself to do some polling, and what I have learned is that there are enough votes among us, which, when added to his own shares will assure that reelection. Do I have a motion for acclamation?"

Phyllis almost missed it, almost missed the fact of what the addition of a few simple numbers would reveal. Distracted by the events of the day, she had forgotten her mother's early telephone call, her only call of the day. Phyllis spoke, "Mr. Chairman, as a voting member of this board, I have a right to call for a count of the votes. I request that count now. I will abstain."

When the votes were tallied, the chair explained, "You see, I was right Phyllis. We conducted the election this way out of concern for you. It seemed prudent. Alec's own shares will assure his reelection."

"Alec has no shares."

The magic of numbers, that progression, the expansion intrinsic in the process of adding one number to a second, to produce a third, a higher number, now revealed a new administrator for the bank. And a future for Phyllis. Keeping her voice low and calm she explained, "The final divorce papers were signed yesterday. All of Alec's shares are now mine and mine alone. Today, my mother sold me her shares. I now own fifty-three percent of the stock in this bank, not one vote of which will support Alec Stockton's presidency."

The chair did not concede gracefully, "But, my dear, Alec was your father's choice! He's been president for years! I cannot believe that he gave up his shares!"

"He wanted a divorce, very much wanted a divorce."

"But there must have been other options."

"I did not need alimony. Besides, he was marrying a stranger."

Understanding the full impact of her words, the chair demanded, "What will he live on? And, he is in debt! To us! Mortgaged himself to buy that house!"

"His wife owns a boutique."

The chair admitted, "We hold the papers on that, also."

"Really!" Having watched many executive games, Phyllis decided to test her own skills. "Perhaps we can offer him something. A teller? Loan officer? No dear, no, not in light of what you have just told me. Maybe a clerk. Or better than that, maybe his wife will hire him."

Flinching from this bit of sarcasm, the chair grumbled, "You are going a little fast for me, Phyllis. We must first name a president." A realist, a polite realist, he asked, "Do you have someone in mind? Maybe one of the junior officers, or, if you prefer, someone new? Maybe a man from one of the branch offices."

"No, none of them." Then she answered everyone's question, "I will be president."

No one objected. No one spoke at all.

Her position made secure by this silence, the silence of respect for money and those who posses it, the new executive addressed her board. "I have been associated with the bank all of my life, and its financial health is important to me. I know that I have your support and cooperation, and I thank you for it. I now adjourn this meeting."

Later, Phyllis instructed her board chairman, "I am certain that Alec will default on those loans, but we will not embarrass a former officer of this institution. They have the boutique, but in the event that they cannot make a reasonable profit, then we will find a manager who can. Maybe mother? She is a good manager."

As Phyllis drove into her garage, her headlights caught the note, a tiny white flag, pinned to the dark plastic. Pocketing the note, she carried her former husband's trash to the curb, left it there for the morning pick-up. Speaking into the dark blueness of the night, she ended her day, indeed, ended an era, "Alec, how careless of you."

babe

"So you're going to Vegas—ever been there? Your first trip? God, ain't that something?—a little more off that left side, Midge, seems to bunch up behind my ear—that's better, good. You'd better watch out for that Gus of yours. He's a good-looking guy, them girls will grab him up in a hurry. Ha, that's a joke. Some of the ones I seen in the two times I been there ain't looking for more men, look worn out with what they already got. Puff it up a little more on the top there, wouldja? Well, as I was saying, I was in the rest room at Caesar's Palace, thought we'd go fancy the last night we was there, and here was one of them girls, cigarette girl or something, forty if she was a day, and with long blond hair. God, they must do a wholesale business in bleach in that town, bleach and make-up! And I asked myself how do they work in them three-inch heels? Well, anyhow, there she was talking to a big fat woman who took care of the toilets—you're supposed to tip to use them places, Midge, might as well know it before you get there. But, as I started to say, this girl in her little bunny suit had to have a hysterectomy, and was she scared! Didn't know nothing about it, hardly knew what it meant, and was she worried! Dabbing at her eye, trying to keep her mascara from running—how'd I get started on this? I know, your Gus. What I mean to say is that if he gets kicking his heels too high, just remember that kid in the rest room. Let him think he's a wild man. You just play the slots and I hope you're lucky. Tell you what, here's a quarter. Play it for me. We'll split if you win a bunch."

That had been Midge's 'two-o-clock' and the first of the lucky quarters. By nine that night she had a pocket full of coins bouncing against her thigh as she cleaned and readied the shop for Wednesday. Exhausted. She still cleaned thoroughly, every box, bottle and instrument in place, every glass surface polished to a hard brilliance, her hands driven by an inner worry. "Just in case." Over and over warning herself, "Just in case," only once finishing with, "In case you're not the one to open it up next time, in case something happens, everything better be right, better be clean, you never know."

Midge's father had built the shop for her, a porch he enclosed. Gus had only grudgingly agreed to having the shop in their home, had muttered warnings about 'devaluating our property' or 'could be a flop', but he did help with some of the inside finishing. Dubbing it 'The Hens' Nest', he disengaged himself from the project, saying, "It's your shot, kid, take care of it." Midge understood him, but she was puzzled, even hurt at times by his remarks, quoted for her by Gertrude, her sister-in-law. "Look, Gert," Midge explained, "we need the money I make and Gus knows that," or "That Gus, he's a regular stand-up comic."

In her kitchen, Midge allowed herself a beer, and an extra Saturday night beer before Gus got home. Chewing on a slice of pizza she found in the microwave, she stretched her legs and crooned to herself, "You're going to Vegas, kid, really going to Vegas! Vegas, the big time!" Gambling was not the 'big time' for Midge. The Vegas that excited her was the city of glamour, glitz, the home of stars, a place where 'even little people like me are welcome'. Midge believed in the Las Vegas touted in her shop magazines and on television that she watched faithfully, the soaps she followed and which Gus ridiculed, insisting that she fell for 'every hunk on the screen'.

"Ain't that a man for you?" Midge had confided to Gert, "Little he knows. He don't know and don't want to know how the really smart people live. But he's wrong, really wrong when he says that's why I watch television. Like I'm some silly kid! How dumb does he think I am?" Midge was shampooing Gert's hair, Gert wincing from the force of the fingers on her scalp. "I just feel good when I watch them, especially the ones about the wrong people having babies, stuff like that, and important people. Like that one the other day where that kid pretended to be a doctor and all the time he was just a phony, I spotted that, and he got what was coming to him. I knew what he was; he had funny eyes, sneaky eyes. And then Gus says I got a thing about doctors!"

"I kinda like the doctor ones," Gert admitted, defending her own prop for facing the world on level ground. "Especially when they're so good-looking. Harry laughs at them. But he's that way when I go to real doctors…I don't know…I don't think I go to doctors that much."

Now, lulled by a beer, Midge planned her own Las Vegas, "What if I would meet a star! Really see one face to face? God! I'll get to see all them places and two shows—topless won't bother me, I ain't never been that goody-goody. And the gambling. I suppose I might, there. What if I'd hit a jackpot! Sweet Jesus! That's a break I could handle...but then there's the flying..."

"Melanie, when the news comes on, I want to hear the weather report. Be sure you call me!"

A girl's voice came from the front room, "Oh, Ma, quit worrying! The weather's all right. Your plane ain't gonna crash, you're just being dumb!"

"All the same I want to hear it! And I want to know if you got your stuff all packed for tomorrow?"

Midge's daughter appeared in the kitchen doorway, "Good God, a person'd think you'd never been any place in your life! And just how long do you think it takes a person to pack for two and a half days? My God!"

"You watch your tongue! I never talked like that when I was your age! Especially not to my mother! And you got so much time, you help Gus Junior with his packing!" Midge was yelling at her daughter's retreating back, "A person'd think you'd be happy your Dad and me got a trip like this, he worked damned hard for it! The least you could do is help! And one more thing, young lady, you'd better mind your Grandmother. You'll find she ain't easy like me!"

And that Grandmother had repeated an old complaint, "Your father and me sitting here on nothing but Social Security." But she would baby-sit, in spite of her, "Me again? How come I'm so privileged? It ain't that I don't love them, but he's got a mother too, you know."

"Ma, she won't let them watch television. They hate that."

"Maybe she's right, all that crime and violence any more. And a little religion wouldn't hurt them, even if it is that stuff she talks about."

"Ma!" Accustomed to her mother's sting, Midge reminded herself, 'She always had to put me through this, but she'd complain if I didn't ask her.' Aloud, Midge offered, "I could leave them home alone. Melanie is fourteen with Harry and Gert so close."

"Me refuse my own grandchildren? What do you think I am made of?" Self-righteously, the older woman ordered, "They'll come here and you just go have a good time. Don't even think of us here at home!"

Midge's kitchen got the same intense cleaning as the shop. She counted off each job as she finished it. At one point she remembered the dog. "That damned dog! He'll just have to go with the kids, or maybe Harry will check on him. Harry! I better call him, Gus would never think to set up a time for tomorrow...no answer...probably still at the golf course, even this late and it dark, probably drinking with their fancy friends. God it would be fun to play golf, dress in them cute outfits, be around them neat people. And Harry's got the money. Started out as a shoe salesman, now look at him…and Gus working like a dog to win this trip, that awful belt, lucky he's still got two hands…but, money!" Her whispers, her happy planning continued until Gus walked in the door, home from his weekend job.

"God, Babe, everybody knows we're going. People asked me about it all day, even old Harry had his two cents worth, stopped for gas this afternoon. They been there three, four, times, told me about all the hot spots, best blackjack and crap tables."

"Gus! You and craps in Vegas? An international place like Vegas?" Midge demanded more than Harry's Vegas, pudgy Harry. "Think of all the big-time gamblers there! You ain't in their league!"

"Come on!" Gus knew his own turf, "I've played craps ever since I was a kid—thought it was part of going to school. Besides, we got these games in the Union rec hall. I ain't no greenhorn!" He grabbed Midge by the waist and swung her around the small kitchen, singing to her, "I'm a winner kid! The winner who's taking you to Vegas!"

In bed later, he whispered, "That ain't all Harry talked about, says it's real easy to get a girl down there."

"Gus!"

"Hold it! I'm just teasing, you're enough girl for me." Then a final tease, sleepily, "Says you can get a man, too, maybe one of them pretty boys."

"You saying that's what him and Gert do down there? God! That's sick! And if you think that's what we're going to do, I ain't going! I am staying right here at home! My god, you really think I'm like that?"

"Don't go nuts! This is the twentieth century, and I'm just telling you what he said." Gus tried to salvage both himself and his brother, "He didn't say they do it, and I ain't saying we should. But you know things are different today—what about those programs you watch all of the time, and the guys the line…"

"Mention it once again, Gus, and I'm not going with you! And maybe you'd better stay home, too! I don't want to even think about things like that! And you got any thinking about another woman, you just let me know! Right now!" Squirming for comfort, Midge scolded with her nose buried in her pillow, "After all these years and…what about AIDS? Don't you know nothing?" She sat up abruptly, "You're damned right this is the twentieth century, AIDS all over the place! And, you get this straight! You want another woman, you're losing this one!"

"Aw, simmer down! Go to sleep!"

Unable to afford clothes for just one trip, and disappointed by Gert, who did not offer to lend some of her expensive clothes—'Harry musta put his foot down, got mean again about her spending so much.' Midge settled for a special hairdo. She searched through trade magazines, television, movies, looking for glamour then got up early Sunday morning to shampoo and dye her hair. She made breakfast, and while Gus drove his family to their Grandmother's house, Midge finished her hair and applied special make-up. She was pleased with her appearance, preened and danced about waiting for Gus to return and tell her she was a knockout.

But Harry and Gert walked in the door with Gus, anxious to pack the bags in the car and be off. No one mentioned Midge's appearance until she was climbing into the car and Harry faked a kiss and whacked her, familiarly, saying, "Ready to go, kiddo? All set for the big Sin City? You ask me, babe, I'd say you're ready for it. You look like a real Vegas filly!"

"Aw, you're always teasing." Then, "Seriously, Gert, what do you think of my hair? You ain't said."

"Oh, God, Midge, it's a...it's great...you do it yourself?"

"Sure, Gert, sure. I could do yours like this, too. You think it's all right, don't you? Too extreme for here, but I thought *Vegas*."

"Oh...yeah. I agree with you, Midge. I do. I do agree with you." Gert looked at Midge's hair closely, "How'd you get them spikes to hold up like that?" Midge stiffened and Gert hurried to say, "That's really a white bleach, really white. Matches your makeup. You get a new line in the shop or something?"

Midge was disappointed, "Well, Gert, if you don't like it, just say so. I picked one of the latest styles, we'll all be looking like this next year." Trying to sound casual, she asked Gus, "You ain't said anything, what'd you think of it?"

Gus, who had not noticed her hair, blurted, "You know me, anything goes. All I know is I'm gonna have a lotta great dames to look at tonight. You're okay."

Harry snorted, "Way to go, kid!"

Gamely, Midge joined the laughter, reminded herself 'Gus and Harry are always like this when they're together. And Gus could have left me home—Harry's done it to Gert often enough.'

For this reason, Midge had not admitted to Gus that she was afraid to fly, had always been afraid of airplanes, having seen one crash when she was a child. 'I'll just stick it out.' She had decided, 'I ain't giving him any excuse to leave me home.' But Harry, thoughtless as usual, spent most of the drive describing air crashes he had seen, terrifying Midge with each gory tale. She was nearly comatose when they reached the airport. Gus, excited himself, ignored her and complained when he had to find their seats himself and insist that she sit down. He growled, "Don't be so damned goofy!"

Midge asked why there was so little room, why they were so far back in the plane. She felt caged, swallowed-up, in the narrow seat, her feet thrust into the only space left above her carry-on. She was barely comfortable when the plane started to taxi, then the noise, the forward thrust, the sight of land falling away immobilized her. She spent the flight braced against the seat, her hands clutching the armrests, and her mind captured by thought of crashing and dying. Dying a painful death. Every swerve and bump of the plane produced a new terror. Gus, quickly tired of her complaints, talked basketball with the man across the aisle.

On the ground after a dizzying descent, Midge left the plane weak, nauseous. She brightened somewhat walking into the baggage room, only to reel anew from the onslaught of the heat outside.

Midge did not take her camera with her when she followed Gus to the casino. She debated about sticking it in her purse where Gus would not see it, but what was the use when any picture she might want to take she'd want him to be in. But after that fuss in their room.

"Why are you taking a picture of the bathroom?"

"Not the bathroom! It's our suitcases. I want a picture of them in this room, especially of the one I borrowed from Ma."

"Jesus Christ! I should have left you home! Quit acting like a damned hick!"

She did take the two-dollar rolls of nickels with her. She had hesitated at first, thinking it would be fun to take home for Gus Junior, but decided that she owed it to the hotel to spend them.

The casino disappointed Midge. The thick carpets, the colors, the movement of lights, the rich décor dazzled her, but there were too many people, too many ordinary people in very ordinary clothes. She had envisioned an intimate atmosphere with recognizable people playing the games, celebrities, glamorous people. She saw no familiar faces, no starts of television or the movies. With some disappointment, she turned to Gus, "There's more people here than live in our whole town!" Gus had vanished.

Alone, she felt shy, worried about 'looking dumb'. Trying to be sophisticated, she talked archly to two women playing slot machines. They ignored her. She wandered through the maze of gamblers hoping to find 'someone nice to visit with', knew she had to be careful. When she found a woman near her own age, she sat on the stool next to her and asked, "Are you here on vacation? Where do you live?" The woman glared at her.

Feeling very alone, Midge broke open a roll of nickels and played the machine in front of her. Like a favored child, she was lucky. In the short time that she had before the supper show, she won nine dollars.

Sadly, his friends at home had failed to tell Gus about the benefits of selective tipping. Midge's quick eyes had seen the green bills proffered to willing hands in the dining room, but Gus was stubborn, "The hell I will! We got paid reservations and that's all they're going to get!"

The cunning Nevadans who lure the Guses and Midges to their tables are generous hosts, their food and service the talk of a continent. Unspoiled by quick-food and catsup-doused concoctions at home, Midge ate and drank everything placed before her. She stuffed herself, became giddy with alcohol, and fell in love with Gus all over again. She saw most of the show in spite of the several heads between her and the stage, and if there was gaudiness and tinsel in the production, she missed it. She was enchanted by the costumes, by the beautiful semi-nude young dancers, and by the music. She beat time to show tunes and wept a little at romantic 'oldies', and she was thrilled by the magnificent sound of an American jazz band, 'in concert'.

Gus was gracious, "Never say I did nothing for you, babe."

After the show, she followed him to a blackjack table and watched while he won forty dollars and then quickly lost fifty. Exhaustion won. He told her, "That's it, kid. I'm too beat to play this one out and we got all of tomorrow. Let's have a look at the night and then hit the hay."

Midge woke alone, Gus wasting no time to prove his skills at the games. She stretched luxuriantly, stroked the bed clothes, her own body, still in the embrace of sleep, but awake, the mattress hardened, the pillows became lumpy, and the bedspread, the room smelled of kerosene from the cleaning spray that had just covered up the body odors, and the grease and the rust of many years. The worst treachery lay in the bathroom mirror. Her hairdo had collapsed, its glamour tumbled away in the night. She brushed, combed, shampooed, but with no luck. She talked at herself in the mirror, "No matter what I do it looks like a bird's nest plopped upside down on your head! It was a dumb idea. I guess you really are a hick from the sticks and right now I wish you had brought your whole damned shop with you!"

With the help of a cleaning girl, she got to the right corner and on the right bus to a mall and bought the hairdressing equipment she needed, but she returned to the hotel with sore feet and a dizzying headache, brought on by a rich dessert for lunch, and the heat outside. She had not seen Gus in all of this time, but while she was working on her hair he appeared, dropped heavily on the bed and asked, "What in hell are you doing to your hair now?"

Midge did not enjoy the dinner show that night. The featured start was an aging country and blues singer with a back-up comedian who told nasty jokes about sex, jokes that Midge did not understand. Gus seemed to as he laughed a lot. Midge had one moment of glory and attention when she caught a red garter thrown into the audience by one of the dancers. She slipped the colorful bit of satin and lace over her knee for luck. It proved to be an unlucky charm, an evil talisman.

Midge faced a lonely evening, Gus wanting, "One big night on my own." She played keno for a while, and the slots. In a later year, wise enough to dress comfortably, she would meld into the impersonality of the crowd and play the slots most of the night. Now, looking for someone to talk to, hoping to find some of the companionship of the places she and Gus frequented at home, she found a bar and ordered a drink. There was no talk, no fun. On her way to an elevator, she saw Gus. He was one of an excited crowd watching the throw of dice down the green lane of a craps table.

Midge watched, then, wanting so much to be part of the excitement, she found a place near Gus, only to be forced back by anxious bettors and the cold stare of the stick man. Frightened by these people who played with money, she worried about Gus, knowing that seven was not a lucky number for him and believing that the figures painted on the green baize top were some mysterious code or message far beyond his understanding. And she feared the dice, believing that they were gypsy-like devices that stole from people and brought them harm.

Gus was fearless when the dice were presented to him, natural and easy in a place so alien to Midge. Her own hoard of fifty dollars was still safe, too hard earned to risk losing. But Gus won, won many times, and then stopped playing. He had won three hundred dollars with the dice.

"Oh, Gus! Three hundred dollars! Now we can be together for the rest of the night!"

But Gus wanted to play poker, "There's a game going on upstairs that I know I can get in."

"Poker! Here? You?" Midge insisted, "This isn't your league, Gus, and we can do a lot with three hundred dollars!"

"Jeez, it's like this, babe, I'm playing for the guys at home. They expect me to. They'll ask me about it when I get back!" He was very sure of himself, "I'll know when to get out, and with three hundred dollars as a cushion, I won't get hurt. Tell you what," he bargained, "we'll spend tomorrow morning together doing the things you want before we have to check out. You look beat. Why don't you go up to bed now? I may be late."

Morning brought a betrayal that nearly shattered Midge's world. She could not rouse a sleep-sodden Gus and went to breakfast alone. When she returned to their room he was on his knees looking under the bed. He admitted that he had lost his billfold. When she demanded to know where he had lost it, where he had been, he recited a gibberish of accusations against the hotel, against the help, against the 'the whole damned town of Vegas, out to get the little guy!' He told her he had been taken at the poker table, made a little, then lost down to about one hundred dollars and quit playing. "I might have dropped it in the room, but I really think I was hustled by the bar maid. We'll never find it!"

Midge insisted that they look for it and wanted to call the front desk to report their loss, but Gus called her a 'dumb little jerk', adding, "This ain't the sticks, kid! We can just kiss it goodbye, money and all!"

She defied him. "I'm going down to the manager's office! I ain't giving up that easy!"

"No!" Gus shouted, but she was gone.

From the manager's office she was ushered into a small room and asked to fill out a questionnaire. Little was said to her, and she began to believe that she might really be that dumb little jerk that Gus had called her, and was surprised when the billfold was thrown onto the table in front of her.

"Where did you find it?" she asked. The clerk ignored her. She found no money in the wallet, only credit cards.

"Better check them credit cards, sister."

A middle-aged man, a gambler, had been watching her, amused by her sincerity and her innocence. He advised her further, "I don't know nothing about where that billfold's been, kid, but you oughta know I had a sleazy little trick out here, take only one of my cards, cost me a bundle before I missed it."

Midge did not understand.

He helped her, "They tell me a piece of plastic is worth a hundred or more on the street here, and for these girls, that's a hundred bucks without working."

"These girls…a sleazy little trick?…Gus and a girl?" Stunned, Midge babbled to herself, 'No, he didn't he couldn't have…but you know he did…please God, not Gus.' The shouted "No!" rang in her ears, and Harry's talk, the guys at work. Gus in Vegas, their guy in Vegas. She'd go to him, ask him, tell him, she'd know the truth by his face, she'd know! But she stopped at the elevator door, turned back to the casino. Stunned, wandering aimlessly, her mind fighting an inner collapse, throbbing from a brutal hurt, Midge faced betrayal, disgust, and the bitterness of an alliance with a 'sleazy little trick—no better than that!' No one noticed her stumbling, her blank stare. She bumped into a stool, sat down and began feeding nickels into the slot, not caring if she won or lost. Gradually, her pull at the arm of the machine stiffened into a jerk, and her thoughts burst into a torrent of words addressed to a contrivance of metal and glass. "He can't have the kids! They don't need something like him for a father! But he'd better support us, he ain't getting by without that, and I've got the shop! I'll show him! I'll fight him!" Searching in her purse for change, she saw the carefully saved tip money. "That's it, by God! I'll spend every damned dime I've got! I may be a dumb bimbo, but I'm no longer an easy one! I'll show him!" She went to the dollar machines.

In a rare streak of contrariness, the system thwarted her. She could not lose. She jammed dollar after dollar into the slot only to have the money flow back. She battled the gaudy computer, spent the money as fast as she won it. Other gamblers drew close to watch, and they shouted in delight when a large jackpot cascaded into her lap. Sobbing wildly, she dumped the money on the floor and left the machine, shouting, "Take it! Take every last dollar of it! I hate this place, hate this awful place!" She faced the people watching her, "Why are you here? Don't you know what this place does to you?"

A woman, a leathery-faced grandmother, stopped her, "Wait a minute, doll, it's your money, take it." She held Midge's arm, looked closely at her and guessed, "This is a man ain't it? Forget him. Ain't a man in the world worth what you're doing." Then she took Midge's purse and held it open while others filled it with recovered winnings.

Midge handed Gus his billfold, saying only, "Better check the credit cards." He did not ask about the purse heavy with silver dolls. They sat in silence for the three hours of their wait at the airport. Once Gus ventured, "Glad to be going home, kid?" No response. He added, "I am. That place was getting to be a little much for a country boy like me…but this country boy's got a lot to tell the guys at home—ain't that right?"

In the plane, Gus asleep beside her, Midge searched, 'There he is, dead to the world, sleeping like a kid. Maybe he didn't do it, or thinks what he did ain't wrong.' She saw an aging Gus, innocent in sleep, one hand lying across her arm. She saw again that hand throwing the dice, 'so great, so excited, and now back to that awful line. I don't know, should I ask him? Find out he didn't and him to believe I thought he did? Or ask him, find out he really did, and then what? Hear him say what I know he'll say. I don't need that, don't need to be told what I am or what I'm not—he's so quick with words. He and Harry, Harry and those guys at work. Sometimes I hate Harry, hate it when he and Gus are so thick. "Propping each other up", Gert calls it…maybe she's right, maybe they do prop each other up, scared, needing so awful much to be what they ain't, and then bouncing their sacredness off on me and Gert.'

Later, when Gus woke, nuzzled his face close to hers and asked, "Love your old man, babe?" she answered, "Sure, Gus."

"God, Midge, here it is a whole week and you been to the big gambling capital of the world and back already, just like nothing had happened! Amazing, ain't it? Did you have a good time? Had a ball, I betcha, didn't I tell you? And it's all over town about all the money Gus won, ain't he the lucky guy! I see you won something too. I was in that place once where they give away them pretty garters, but I wasn't close enough or lucky enough to catch one, but it looks cute up there. You can see two of them, caught on the edge of the mirror like that. Bet you put it there to remind yourself of all the fun you had. It's kinda like a good-luck charm too, ain't it? Bunch it up like last week."

Mater Misericordiae

Mike Jensen rubbed the circulation back into his stinging fist as he circled his truck, checking each tire with a short, measured kick, a ritual reassurance. The night was warm, but dark and starless. The only light came from the kitchen of Mike's house. He ran his hand over the supplies that he had carefully stowed in the back of the truck, stood for a moment, watched his house until it, too, became dark, then he pulled himself up into the cab of the truck and proclaimed to the night, "Damned Women! Never know when to shut up! Never know when to let go of a man!"

The truck was old, worn out, one that Mike had bartered for, a necessity in cashless times. He had traded his labor on an old reject parked in a junkyard. Carefully, painstakingly he had tuned it, greased it, found parts for it, and literally willed it into use. Now, close to midnight, his skirmish with his wife behind him, he skillfully coaxed a motor into life, gave it full throttle for a few minutes, and then eased the old dray out onto the cobblestone street.

In the embrace of the darkness, the stillness, he began the night's venture. The weak headlights revealed little of the road ahead, and the yellow streetlights were mere dots against the heavy blackness. And no light from the houses, those dark bulky shapes huddled together, clinging to the sides of the hills, their inhabitant born too soon for the forty-hour week and cheap electricity. No vehicles lined the streets, which faithfully followed the contour of the land and led Mike up and down steep hills, hills that strained both the motor and the brakes of the old vehicle. He avoided the worst of the hills and twice lost his way to detours, causing a late arrival at the apartment building where a man waited, standing in the darkened doorway of the barbershop that was tucked into the small space between a pool hall and a neighborhood grocery store.

As he slammed the door of the truck, Ranse turned on Mike, "Where the hell you been? I been standing there for an hour—that woman of yours give you trouble?"

Mike lied, "Naw, it's the truck. She's slow on the hills."

"Well, keep her moving, we got a lotta hills ahead of us." His voice was demanding, staccato-like, "You know how to get there? We gotta come in from the alley."

So the journey started with the truck first rattling through the downtown district, now abandoned for the night with empty streets and few lights. The road led up into a new set of hills, with Mike instinctively gunning the motor past the hospital perched like a brooding matriarch on the city's highest point. Mike saw hospitals as places of death.

After several blocks more Mike left the paved road to make a sharp turn into an alley. He stopped the truck near the back door of what looked to be a warehouse. He had turned the headlights off, but he found his way well enough to park backwards, ready for a quick getaway.

The neighborhood was new to Mike, and he was worried, worried about being caught and then arrested, worried about Ranse's crazy notions, notions that frequently meant bad trouble. He stepped down from the truck slowly, and before releasing the door handle he pleaded with Ranse.

"D'ye really want to go through with this?"

A whispered command, "Dammit, shut up! You'll wake the whole town!"

"I said, shut up! Here, gimme that flashlight, see if that window is locked!"

The owner of the building had made little provision to keep anyone out, and the two men were soon inside to begin their search. The strange acrid odor of the room bothered Mike, took his breath and made him nauseous. He waited as Ranse moved ahead into a large storage area. The place had a spooky color, everything in the room painted white, so much white that it seemed to glow from within itself. Ranse played the light back and forth across this whiteness, giving the room an illusion of motion, a movement accented by objects that seemed to appear and disappear as the light played across their surfaces. Breathless and on the verge of panic, Mike pressed the palms of his hands against the cool wall. His head reeling, he pressed closer and closer to the wall, then relaxed and slid quietly to the floor.

Ranse's voice came to him from far off. Slaps on his face were coaxing him nearer consciousness. "Jesus Christ! Are you all right? That's all I need, you passin out on me! Are you all right? Get up! Dammit, get up!" The furious whispers, the slaps, and two strong arms forced Mike to his feet. He moaned, "God, Ranse, ain't you scared of nothing?"

Ranse ignored him, ordered, "Get over here! Grab that end!" The two men lifted a woman's body from one of the tables and started for the door. Mike had a second horrible moment when the sheet slipped and his hand closed on cold, dead flesh.

Ranse screamed, "Dammit! Watch it! Them stitches won't hold if we drop her!"

"Jesus, Ranse!" Mike blurted, "don't be so damned jumpy! You know I never done nothing like this before!"

Once outside, safe at the truck and in the darkness, the men worked quietly with Mike calm and sure of himself. Ranse followed his orders. Their cargo secure, they started the motor, and began the race, the hoped-for escape, the flight homeward. The truck chugged quietly down the alley and out into the street again, now heading for the state line and Jennings County. They had chosen the Hawkins Hill road as there were only a few houses along it, and it was closest to the highway from this side of town. It also had the most hills.

Mike was a good driver, but Ranse repeatedly warned that they were lost, that each turn was a mistake, that the truck would never make it over the next hill, and that Mike never did nothin' right. Throughout their long friendship, Mike had learned to ignore Ranse when he talked 'so blameful, like somethin' was drivin' him.' Mike had made this trip at night before and probably would again, many times, as his friends in Jennings County could not afford to buy any vehicle and hired others to carry their home-brewed whiskey out of the state for shipment to Chicago. The week previous to this Mike had earned fifteen dollars, which he had used to buy a license for the truck. "The damned government fifteen dollars you to death," he sympathized with Ranse, but he could not risk being caught without a license when ferrying whiskey. In truth, Mike feared the country officers more than he feared the fledgling federal officers.

Soon dense undergrowth and weedy ditches indicated that they were now outside of the city limits. Steep hills lay ahead, hills thick with trees whose heavy branches spread across the road in places to form dark tunnels. Mike knew that he must watch carefully for turns, for sudden downhill runs and twisting climbs back up. The road was not new to him, but there was wickedness in the night. And if Ranse had been driving, the ride past the cemetery would have been uneventful, but Mike had not been raised in a home where the prospect of death was part of life. Mike dealt with death from a distance, and only in daylight, and mostly with his own primitive imagination. He always hurried past cemeteries. He believed that they were places of ghosts and of evil spirits buried deep. He heard about them at funerals and was convinced that they were always trying to get out of those deep holes, and that night was the best time for them. Just as the headlights caught the first grave marker, a low-hanging branch scraped across the hood and rose up over the cab of the truck. Mike, however, saw a giant black ant grabbing for the corpse that they had stolen, had stolen to escape its burial in that very cemetery. Mike bolted. The truck leapt into the darkness, to shoot up hills and race down, its tires touching the road only to spew a storm of dust and gravel into the fiery wake of the exhaust.

Ranse's screams saved them from flying over a steep embankment. Mike braked to an abrupt stop, only to hear, "You Goddamn crazy fool! You can't even drive!"

Sheepish and shaken by the near disaster that his 'crazy imaginins' had caused, Mike drove on slowly, forced himself to think of nothing but the road ahead. Only when beyond the grove of trees where the road leveled off to approach the interstate bridge, did Mike loosen his grip on the steering wheel, stretch his cramped legs, and recover a sense of 'rightness', and once again be the agent of justice for the needy. The truck slipped between the narrow side rails into Jennings County. What neither man knew was that the wild ride in the hills had avenged the world of the dead. A rope holding the body had broken.

Tired from the hour of the night and free of the strain of their activities, they now relaxed as they crossed bottomlands on a rutted gravel road, the main highway in this lush farm country. There was no traffic and no lights on the horizon except those coming from buildings nestled at the ends of long lanes, dots of light from kerosene lamps in farmhouses built well away from the highway.

Ranse broke the silence, "What in hell got into you back there?" He charged at Mike. "You damned near killed us!"

With innate self-respect, Mike lied, "Oh, the gas feed sticks once in a while. I'll get around to fixing it. Hey, look, here comes a car."

"Keep on going!" Ranse barked, "The sheriff won't be here, he keeps to the side roads for what he's looking for."

"I know that," Mike grunted, "Jesus!"

They were safe. The car passed them and did not stop, and did not turn around to come back. A little ashamed of their reproaches of each other, both men were silent for a long time. In the quiet they became aware of a movement, a noise in the back of the truck, a bumping sound, a swishing sound, a sound more felt than heard above the noise of the motor. Ranse was certain that they had a flat tire, had 'known all along' that Mike would do 'some dumb thing to mess us up.'

"Why in hell don't you ever get some decent tires on this old heap? You never do anything right!"

The injustice of this accusation did not occur to Mike, but he did not think that a flat tire was the cause of the bumps. He drove more slowly; found a farm lane with the house deep enough within the land that a parked truck would not be noticed. Ranse's cursing at Mike stopped when they saw the back of the truck. Cautious use of the flashlight spared them much of the ghoulish sight that the wild ride in the hills had precipitated. The body, torn out of the blankets and held by only one strand of rope, had been thrown back and forth across the bed of the truck. With urgent whispers and in the dark they retied the frayed rope gathered the dusty blankets and once again covered the corpse from the eyes of a greedy world. Ranse had to force a stiffening leg into realignment.

Jocko Finnegan was pleased with himself. Loaded with whiskey from his up-county farm, he had filled the gas tank of his new Chevrolet and boldly taken the longer main road toward the state line, planning to make a last minute detour and cross on the abandoned middle bridge just above the village of Garry. He did not drink when he was delivering whiskey to the Chicago connection, but this night he was intoxicated with his own cleverness, the feel of his fine new car on the road, and the sound of his own tenor voice, but nearly a mile after passing Mike's truck the singing stop. He swore to himself.

"Holy Mother of God!"

Any reminder of death while transporting whiskey would have frightened most of the bootleggers in Jennings County. Surreptitious activities intensified their already superstitious natures. They had no moral qualms about making the whiskey, but marketing it illegally was a dangerous game. Any sign of death would have sent most of them scampering home to hide the liquor until a safe market materialized, a market with no otherworld manifestations. Unlike most of these entrepreneurs, Jocko was not a married man with children to support. He could afford to take chances. He was making money, a great deal of money, in times when the need for cash compromised many men—those who made the whiskey and those who betrayed friends by helping the police find their stills. Jocko outwitted both these traitors and the police. He had no respect for them. Physically he was not afraid of any man, nor was he intimidated by the legal ramifications of bootlegging. He knew that Prohibition was man-made, and thus was insignificant when compared to the real law, the word of God. Jocko carried God's presence with him constantly; talked to Him, bargained with Him, knew that ultimately everything that happened for good or ill lay in his hands. Now, like a banshee's warning, the dead woman's leg, bouncing over the side of the truck, was a sign from Him, a serious holy sign.

Jocko hated confession, God, how he hated confession. But he feared Hell too much to gamble with his own soul. Twice a year he honored a pact with the Church and his mother and went to confession, and the next day approached the communion rail as the pious penitent made new, the devout Catholic, the community man. But on a country road, in the middle of the night in August—August four months since the Easter confessions and four months yet to go until Christmas—Jocko wisely assessed the state of his own soul. Was he ready to face God and His judgment? The absolute, rock-bottom truth was that no absolution could last four months. He could not risk it. As he examined his conscience, Jocko's spiritual concern deepened. He was bootlegging in the time of the Great Depressions, a time of hunger and suffering, and of ignorance. The zealous parish priests who dealt with these conditions preached the need for humility and the acceptance of God's will, Sunday after Sunday, season after season. These sermons had taken their toll: Jocko was guilty of success. For years he had accommodated these priests, had knelt in the confessional in the posture of a poor man pursued by the law. In the confessional he actually believed that he was a poor man pursued by the law. In the confessional he did not separate a spiritual posture from the truth, but, now stricken honest by a sign from the dead, Jocko knew that the Chevrolet and the whiskey in its trunk made him a liar, a liar before God, the God of the poor, of the suffering, the only God that Jocko knew.

This Irish bootlegger heroically absolved himself. His act of contrition on this night was an offering of wine, wine returned to the Earth from whence it had been given him.

Alerted by the noise of the car, most of the crickets, frogs, snakes, and insects inhabiting the ditch had scurried away. The slower, smaller animals drowned in the distilled grain. Those who escaped did not return until the soil had absorbed and neutralized the ascetic purity of the corn liquor.

Mike and Ranse had planned their trip with care and were able to drive through the main street of a small town and into the backyard of a shabby house well before daylight. An older man, pushing his nightshirt into the top of his trousers came out of the house, and the three men tenderly carried the body though the kitchen and into the bedroom off the parlor. They returned to the truck and neatly rolled the old blankets and ropes so that Mike could put them in the cab. The young woman who had been crying in the kitchen came out and offered to wash the blankets. Mike shook his head, but he did accept her offer of breakfast.

The men sat down to a meal of thick mush, coffee, and slabs of homemade bread. Ranse liked his father-in-law's house, the plainness and simplicity of life appealed to him. His sister-in-law worked in one of the stores in town to support herself and her father, but her kitchen was always clean, uncluttered, not like the kitchens of his own sisters. He had once said to one of them, "You're like a damned pack rat, Lottie. You never let go of anything, savin' everything you ever owned and always grabbin' for more." Now hungry and tired, he needed both the food and quiet of this room. Pouring coffee for the second time, his father-in-law spoke, "Do you want me to call Father Connors, Ranse?"

"I suppose so."

"Is it all right if we bury her next to her mother? In the Protestant cemetery?" The older man knew that Ranse could not afford a grave plot, but he knew that there would be trouble from Ranse's family.

"Yes, don't listen to Connors." Ranse got up quickly and went into the bedroom where his sister-in-law had nearly finished washing the corpse.

"She's pretty badly beaten up, Ranse. You should've called me for the money."

"You keep your money, besides, I wanted to bring her myself." In this house, Ranse's decisions were respected, but out of long habit, conditioned in the past, the need to justify himself made him add, "I've always hated those spooky-looking undertakers." Then he asked, "Do you think the one here will get nosy? What'll you say about the scratches and bruises? And about how she got here?"

"He's so greedy for money that he'll grab that county check and ask no questions. I can handle him."

Together they turned the body over, and she began to arrange the tousled hair.

"Did she die hard, Ranse?"

"Hard enough."
"Was Lottie there?"
"No."
"Does she know you were bringing her here?"
"No."
She shuddered, "Do you want me to call..?"
"I'll do it."
"Don't be too hard on her, Ranse, she only did what she thought she had to. I wish it could have been a nicer wedding, but she did have one, and it's all right; the funeral is going to be in the Catholic Church. Somehow they seem to make everything important. Even burying you."

I suppose I'll cry again, you'd think once you'd cry and get it over with, but it don't work that it keeps comin and comin and I look so awful with my face screwed up and red—damn that Julia makin fun of me and not a tear on her face—she's too mean to cry, always thinking she's better'n the rest of us; her nose up in the air, her snooty bridge playing friends know she's never had fifteen dollars to give anybody and all that talk all the way over about how awful and good-fer-nothin he is and she's so ashamed of him, her own brother. Oh, God, the poor devil, why didn't he call us? I'da got the money for him some way even if we had to borrow it....spose I made him mad callin' the priest but I couldn't let her die with a sin like that on her soul and I don't care if I did make him mad; it was for his own good, he knew he was living in sin with her only a justice-of-the-peace marryin' them, he shoulda married her long ago. Every time I'd say something, I'd get a smart answer from him telling me he wasn't sure to live with her all of his life, well God sure took him at his word, he found out and Father said I was right, he oughta known I wouldn't do something like that without finding out first—many is the time I've had to go to him and this time he said yes, you've got to go, you mustn't let her die without the marriage being blessed by the Church; he's committin' a terrible sin. He's losin' his soul and Father's so good driving me all the way down there in his nice car and now she'll get a good Church funeral and he can start goin' to church again, maybe stop drinkin' too...I just can't understand it, he's ruinin' himself with it, but she never seemed to mind...I'da killed him, I'da broke him of that damn drinking if it was the last thing I ever did...I really don't think Pa was like that but both the boys 'n he's just like Joe, get him a good job and the first thing you know, he's lost it drinkin' and then he's crawlin' back to you like a baby, I wonder what he'll do now, he's no good alone. I wish I could stop thinking about him it's like his face is plastered all over the inside of my head, those black curls and those blue eyes always jumpin', always looking for trouble and finding it time and again. She'd spank him, make him promise to be good, but he's so stubborn he wouldn't cry not even that time she took the stick to him for skippin' Catechism, wouldn't Julia be the one to find him downtown and then tattle to Mama about it. Always was a damn tattletale, but we fixed her. I'll bet she thought twice before takin' her pants down in the weeds again, and that Hank Neguard struttin' around the bank like butter wouldn't melt in his mouth...I don't suppose he'll go back there; probably owes everybody he knows and now the doctor and the hospital. God I hope I never have to go to that place again how she cried when she found out she was gonna die, the tears rolling down her face and him like a kid blubberin' there beside her no good to her at all at least he went to confession, spose it was the first time in years always said he hated priests could live without their hell and mortal sin well he's sure made his own hell, trouble is he could be so good us stealin' watermelons and I was so scared old man Rilery nearly caught us, imagine using a shotgun like that and us layin' in the ditch he nearly suffocated me with his hand over my mouth me cryin' but he had me laughin' before we got to the barn always was good for a laugh, oh, Ranse, Ranse it hurts just to think of you if only alcohol had never been invented where is he now I hope he's not drunk and I don't see him and I don't think I can go in that house I can't look at her and Julia will act like she's the Queen of Sheba talking down her nose to everybody I always feel like such a damn kid around her...they must hate us I don't even speak to the sister on the street her and that no-good bum of a Jake Thorne him with a wife of his own but she does work hard look at her now she scares me seems to look right through me—

"Yes, she was too young to die, but the doctor said when he opened her up, she was just full of it."

—it takes all kinds, there's some flowers some of them home grown hope there's some masses Oh God I'm gonna be sick what'd he do to her look at her the marks are comin' through the powder eternal-rest-grant-unto-her-oh-Lord-   and-let-perpetual-light-shine-upon-her-may-her-soul-and-all-the-souls-of-the-faithful-departed-through-the-mercy-of-God-rest-in-peace-mercy-of-God-mercy-of-God-eternal-rest-grant-unto-her-oh-Lord-oh   that awful emptiness pushin' up from my insides and let-perpetual-if I could just hang on to something—light-shine-Julia's not even bothered upon-her-soul-and-all-the-souls-you'd think she was the Blessed Virgin herself talking to God of-the-faithful-departed -rest-in-peace-she don't fool me none looking so pious she's getting her licks in for her own grand reception…I'm getting sicker maybe I'd better say a Hail Holy Queen it always makes me feel good Mother-of-mercy-our-life-our-sweetness-our-hope-God don't let me fall don't let me touch that coffin to-thee-do-we-cry-to-thee-do-we-sigh-poor-banished-children-of-Eve-banished children…to-thee-do-we-sigh, I mean send up our sighs-mourning-and-weeping-that's me-in-this-vale-of-tears-tears-tears-oh Ranse how could you do it oh-clement-oh-loving-oh-sweet-Virgin-it's no good the words don't change nothing and I'm so ashamed she never hurt anyone in her life and now she looks so awful it didn't help her none to be so good and she didn't know better than to live with him the way she did seems funny you can't love somebody right without first getting on your knees and blabbin' all your secrets but he knew he always knew that that's the way it has to be she taught him that it'd sure be a lot easier if you didn't have to think so much about what happens after you die but you just can't take chances but I don't know she's in heaven or hell or purgatory or just dead dead dead I'd just once like to see that eternal light shinin' over us and not be worried that they're just damn words and nobody really knowin'…'cept there's gotta be something this ain't enough and I can't think I won't ever see her or any of the others again and after trying so hard to do the right thing you know there's gotta be something and sometimes in dreams there's such a good feeling you're sure there's something good waiting for you…I just can't imagine it though they talk about God on a throne and all the business of the order of the angels and that stuff suppose it'll be just my luck to be wanderin' around at the bottom someplace, another kid up there with Julia higher'n me clicken' her beads all over the place Hail-Mary-Holy-Mary- Hail-Mary-Holy-Mary, hell'd be better than that down there burnin' I wonder why they tell you about the fires in hell when they know you won't have nobody how'll you feel it? I spose that's that mystery Father is always talking about, he knows, he's gotta know, somebody's gotta know but sometimes I want to say you can have your damned old mysteries just somebody once tell me why I feel so bad so much why I cry so much why I'm cryin' now cryin' for him instead of her because I guess that's what I'm really doing and why every time I kneel here when somebody dies I feel the same way I always end up the same old way knowin' only to say the same old prayers the old Hail Marys like a kid runnin' to its mother Hail-Mary-full-of-grace-Holy -Mary-Mother-of-God-pray-for-us-sinners-now-and-at-the-hour-of-our-deaths- Amen-I guess I feel better at least I've quit cryin' he still hasn't come you'd think just once he could do like other people I'll have to find him who'll I ask?

"He's in the back yard, Lottie."

She walked slowly through the kitchen and crossed the weedy backyard. Pride salvaged, anger spent Ranse waited for her, sitting on a bench in the shade of an old maple.

Dry-eyed, her own doubts and grief resolved by the vigil at the casket, Lottie found a narrow path through the long, dry grasses and walked steadily toward Ranse. When he saw her approaching, he doubled over in sobs.

Lottie sat down on the bench, close to Ranse, and wept with him.

The Shrinks, A Love Story

"I watch you, see you working so hard, so careful with the dishes, the rug."

She kept her eyes lowered as she brushed crumbs onto a soiled linen napkin, and smoothed wrinkles from the tablecloth. Had she heard him?

'Lord, help me,' he prayed. A timid man, he saw himself as a poor show in God's scheme of the world, and, the problem before him now, as God's test of his worthiness. Relying on God's grace, he spoke courageously.

"I think you like your work, like doing God's work in this way, and with Rusty so happy here, his education to be taken care of. That was a promise. Have you decided yet?"

"No, father." She tried not to hate him, hate him for reminding her of what she must do, hate him for dragging his truth into her life, towing truth with him everywhere in his simple and clumsy way. Buster running off again, the rent not paid, no food. Now this. She would thank him to keep his truth. She just wanted to be here, safe, for as long as she needed this house, this living, Rusty with her. Now this change. Damn the Bishop.

Her movements were hurried, brisk, efficient, the softness gone from her face, every shred of gentleness or weakness drawn within her and held there fiercely. She worked like one bent to the whims of an unseen taskmaster. Unseen, not this pious and quiet man, worrying about her tomorrow.

Later, she told her sister Nell, "Him sitting there like a big overgrown kid, don't he know I couldn't pay for anything I might break—that Altar Society, Gen Murphy, so damned important, always nosing around, always whining, 'Be careful with the dishes, Jay, you know howl long we worked for the money to buy them'. I'd like to drop a plate on her head!"

"Think of it as a promotion, Jerry," the Bishop had consoled the sad looking man sitting before him, "the parish you now have is little more than a mission, and there are a hundred families where I am sending you, much more responsibility, and, I believe, a means for spiritual growth for you."

"Yes, Excellency."

The Bishop waited. He had not expected the profuse gratitude of an ambitious man or the groveling humility of a man being reprimanded, but he had hoped for more than this silent abjection, which was disturbing. What had he missed?

Perhaps his family. "I have talked to your mother, and she did not seem to be unhappy about this move. I know that she has enjoyed having you so close to her, but she is a good Catholic mother and understands the ways of the Church, the ways of God."

"She bought me a new car."

"Ah-h, yes, of course…I know of her generosity, her great charity…toward the Church." His authority challenged once more by this mother, the prelate managed only a terse, "The diocese, of course, cannot afford cars for its clergy."

Naïve, good-hearted, the man now being promoted was not aware of the power struggle between his mother and his Bishop to whom he now offered the explanation, "I believe she thinks I'll get home oftener."

Bombardment. First, the housekeeper, now the car. But the decision had been made, other priests had been told of their new assignments, and, transfers should not require a second audience. Searching for enlightenment, the Bishop suddenly remembered the rumors, the speculations that at the time he had dismissed as ludicrous. Perhaps he had been hasty.

"You have a housekeeper?"

"Yes, Excellency."

"Will she go with you on this new assignment?"

"I have offered her the job, asked her to go with me, her and the boy."

"And?"

"She has not given me an answer. I cannot insist."

"Nor should you." Housekeepers frightened the Bishop. They lacked the obedient spirit of the nuns and had a disarming trick of resorting to motherliness, always at cross-purposes with the dedicatory nature of the priesthood. Often they were argumentative and demanding, particularly about conditions in the church and the parish house. This one had a child, which presented the additional danger of divided loyalties.

"I want you to consider making a change in your domestic situation. I find that it is easier to make such a change at the time of a transfer. It may be kinder then."

Silence. The Bishop tried a sterner approach. "I remind you that for a priest, celibacy never goes unchallenged".

No response. No protestation of innocence.

The Bishop spoke firmly, "Is your housekeeper young? Attractive?" The man facing him looked shocked.

The prelate recognized innocence. And his own limitations. Let God work in His own way.

"Jerry, Father Burns is hearing confessions in the cathedral chapel. I suggest that you seek His grace."

Father Burns' voice was somewhat breathless, "*In nominee Patri et filli...*"

She found more rocks in the driveway and carried them in her skirt. She had made a pocket by holding the hem of her dress up over her stomach. She ran quickly to the shady place in the bushes where she was building a house. If her mother saw her, she would scold about soiling her dress and showing her bloomers, which was silly because they covered her almost to her knees and looked just like her dress. The sewing lady had made them both the same day. She wished that Rusty would come, because then Aunt Jay might give her one of his overalls and they would play together, climbing over things as boys always do, things you couldn't do with a dress on, but things that girls like to do just as much as boys do.

If only he would come. She was tired of playing by herself. All the way in the car she had thought about being with him. He was older than she was, but not even by a whole year. She had lots of cousins, and liked them all, liked her girl cousins when they weren't taking care of her or expecting that she take care of them. She liked her boy cousins, but Rusty best of all. He was not all of the time punching at her with his fists or chasing her and tackling her as some of them did, or laughing at her which made her cry. Rusty should be here now. She was tired of being alone and she needed to ask him if he knew why Aunt Jay cried so when she was talking to her mother.

When they first came, everything was all right. Aunt Jay and a man they called Father were trying to get wax off some candlesticks, big tall candlesticks, almost as tall as she was, and they had piles of wax, all melted and stuck to their bottoms. He told Aunt Jay, "We must not scratch the metal." They were working by the basement door of the church where there was a wall for sitting and for holding in the dirt around a big cistern. All of it was shaded, kept cool, by the tall brick walls of the church.

Then the Father said, "Come with me and maybe we can find one of your Aunt Jay's cookies. Maybe Rusty will show up and have one with us."

She could not understand how anyone like the Father, somebody who liked cookies as well as he did, could break anything, like she heard her grandmother say to her mother, "A priest breaking up a marriage? That's nonsense, Nell, and you know it!" Her grandmother had sounded real cross. They were talking about Aunt Jay so she guessed that it was the same thing that made Aunt Jay cry today and tell her mother, "He's all I've got and what would become of him?" It was something about Rusty's daddy, Uncle Buster.

When she asked her mother about what was breaking all that she said was that Rusty might be moving a long way away from them.

Grown-ups are hard to understand. Where is Rusty? If he'd come maybe he could tell her what was being broken. Maybe if she was real quiet, she could play close to her mother and Aunt Jay. Maybe they wouldn't notice her and she would hear them and find out what was breaking that could hurt so, and send Rusty far away from her.

"Bless me, Father, for I have sinned."

A long pause. Father Burns waited, waited for some time before prompting the penitent, "Do you have something to confess?"

"I'm too fat."

"Yes, but...what I don't...why do you confess that as a sin? It's hardly a matter of grave concern."

"It's a sin of gluttony."

"Perhaps." Puzzled, the confessor wondered why he had been summoned from his studies to confess obesity. Excess weight, a spiritual offense? He doubted that. Perhaps the problem was spiritual quilt, "Have you confessed this sin before?"

"Several times."

"Yes?"

"I make promises to God; over and over I make these promises, but I fail. I am just as fat as ever. I am weak, and I have begun to fear the confessional."

"Have you tried penance?"

"I run a mile a day and offer it to God."

"Quit eating so much. Tell your housekeeper not to cook so much."

"No."

Rank disobedience. Father Burns meditated for several minutes, in a spiritual dilemma. As ordained by God, the confessional was a sanctuary, and its divine purpose must not be given over to the trivia of gossip, but he had heard the rumors, nagging questions about this particular woman that gave cause for concern, concern for the penitent's eternal salvation. He asked, "Are you afraid of this woman?"

"No. I am not afraid of her. I just refuse to tell her not to do what she does so well. She is not to blame for my weight."

"Fire her."

"Fire her! Why?"

"Because your compassion is misplaced and you could be in some danger." Father Burns surprised himself, but he continued, "You may be endangering your immortal soul. You may be blind to the power this woman has over you."

"She has no power. She is poor and needs to work, needs the money she makes. She is supporting a child. Besides that, I hardly see how I could be the one to fire her as my mother pays her salary."

"Your mother! Oh, Jer—," Father Burns stopped, a token of respect for the anonymity of the confessional, and the fact that he had just remembered a second, more immediate concern. The Bishop had phrased it, "Delicacy please, Father." At stake? A debt-ridden dioceses and a wealthy woman proud of her charities.

"We are wasting time. I do not believe that this is a spiritual problem. Have you anything more to say?"

"I believe that God is testing me with this woman."

"Testing you!—How?"

"I believe that God has put her in my care, that He has made me responsible for her."

"How can that be? She has a husband, doesn't she? Where is he?"

"I don't know, and I fear for her."

"Fear what?"

"I think when he is home he beats her."

"That is not your problem! You assume too much! You are guilty of spiritual arrogance, God would never..."

The penitent rallied, cut short the harangue, "Don't bring pride into this! Just give me my penance, and let's get out of here!"

"Gladly! Run an extra half-mile, once a week. Now make a good Act of Contrition."

"Ma, what's going on? Bill called me. He saw Pa getting arrested! What's hap…turn off that damned noise!" Gertrude strode into the room, snapped off the radio and shouted, "Why do the police have my father?"

"Gertrude, you always get so worked up. Calm down!"

"Calm down? My father dragged through the streets by the police and I'm supposed to calm down?"

"Yes. And stop yelling at me." The older woman reached toward her radio, "You want to yell at somebody, you go yell at Nell—she's the one that went crazy and called them! And turn that thing back on! I'm in the middle of a program!"

"Nell? Why would Nell call the police? What's Pa done?"

Lila, the youngest of the sisters, walked into the room and interrupted the conversation, "Oh, Gert, you hear about Jay stealing the priest's car?"

"She never did no such thing! How could it be stolen when was sitting right there! Right in plain sight!"

Gertrude stared at her mother, "Where in plain sight?"

"Nell's backyard, wasn't it Lila?"

"That's what the cops told pa." Lila sat down. She knew the signs, could tell when Gert was 'winding up for a good one'.

Gert obliged her, demanded, "If Jay stole the car, why are they arresting Pa?"

"Are you so God-almighty sure that they are arresting him? You come in here, screaming your head off…"

Gert, wildly, "Ma! What in hell is going on?—Lila, can you make any sense out of this?'

"All I know about Jay is that she took my only suitcase, came and got it in the middle of the night."

"The middle of the night? Rusty! Where's Rusty? I suppose she left him, stole the car and abandoned the kid, just like her! Where is she—and where's your grandson? My nephew!"

"Oh, Gert, you do go on. Rusty's all right. When they stopped here, he was asleep in the backseat of Buster's car, all wrapped up in a blanket."

"Buster's car!" Shock and suspicion collided in Gertrude's mind. "When did Buster get a car? And how? Stole one, I suppose. Some old wreck!" Gertrude was screaming again, "And you let your daughter and your grandson go off with him! Nothing but a damned crook! And he'll kill them! Driving the way he does!"

"Keep it going, Gert! Like always, thinking up all the bad things you can!"

"That's a lie! A damned rotten lie! You do this to me, Ma, do it every time! I try to be decent, try to have a nice house, be somebody, be good to you and Pa," Gert's voice broke, "but it's always her! Dear little Jay! Her or your fancy Nell! Nell lording it all over the rest of us and you let her do it! Like now—sitting there while she sets the cops on my father!"

Tears flowed from Gertrude's eyes. Lila thought they were genuine. She could usually tell when Gert was faking.

"With you, it's always been Nell! Nell or Jay! Jay and the damned bum she married! If he's not in jail, he's drunk, or beating her up!" Gert's voice broke, "The rest of us have to live in this town, too, you know!"

"You stop right there! You wait one blessed minute! He never beat her up! Never!" This gatekeeper, guardian of family pride, demanded, "Tell me one time!"

"What about the black eye last winter? She had to plaster make-up on it for weeks! And he lost his job over it! Remember? That one at Carew's!"

"You forget the six stitches they took in his scalp! God knows what she hit him with! And of course he lost his job! You just don't parade family affairs where you work!"

"You're doing it again!" Gertrude wailed, "Bailed him out of jail and didn't even tell us! Nell had to figure that one out!"

"He really wasn't in jail. And Nell would do well to mind her own business." Emphatically, but patiently she continued, "Besides, it was only fifty dollars. They'd a locked him up all weekend if we hadn't a done it!"

Gertrude rallied, "Only fifty dollars! Sure! So where are they now? Where? And, is my father to be thrown in jail for those two! Cover it up if you must, but what about that poor priest? As good as he was to her, and then she pulls this. And you sitting there pretending it's all right!"

The mother rose from her chair. "Nothing will do, will it, but I tell you the whole story. You won't be satisfied 'till you hear every word! Can't leave nothing alone!"

She glared at her two daughters, "Your problem is that the two of you don't know nothing about the way people think! Nothing at all! And Nell is just as bad!"

Silenced, belittled, scorned, the two women stared at her, braced themselves for the next volley.

"The one thing we can count on with Nell is that she'll blab this all over town. Maybe, for once, she'll be smart and doctor it up a little. Trim it down. Her and her big mouth!"

At times, actually frequently, this latter-day oracle of the hearth, justified her pronouncements, her meddling, with the words, "This family would go to hell in a hand basket if somebody didn't take charge!" Her husband always nodded his head in agreement. Now, fired by the drama of scandal and by the obligations of motherhood, she enlightened her daughters, "About that car. She and Rusty drove it down here last night. She swore to God that the priest let her take it."

"And you believed her!"

"Of course I believed her! And if she had any plans for getting the blasted thing back, I didn't hear them. I suppose that's what the police are doing with your Pa. Nell, of course, couldn't wait, think a little, had to lose her mind, just like you two. So there, that's it. There's your big exciting story about Jay stealing a car, and the police being called."

Gertrude recognized the dismissal. Not Lila.

"Gert's right. You can be damned awful partial, Ma. And you've always protected her."

"Protected who?"

"Jay! You're doing it right now, aren't you? You know she's blown it! Walked away from the best job she ever had, that priest so good to her and all! But off she goes—and where are they now? Where is Jay right now! And how did he find her this time?"

"I don't know. Only they can tell you that. I just know that everything's all right with them. They are going to be fine. Buster promised me that!"

Turning back to her radio, she offered a benedictory. "You ask me where are they are. All I know is what Buster said. He told me they're going to Texas, maybe California. Told me he'd get rich in the oil fields in Texas. Didn't say how he'll get rich in California."

The Delousers, They Who Know Where the Bananas Are

"No after dinner cigar, George."

George Leadwell suddenly understood, understood all, opened parlor doors, opened parlor windows, new air, readiness of the house for company. He extinguished the match in his hand and returned the cigar to an inner coat pocket, "The ladies of the LTA?"

"Yes, and you know Hattie Smith could smell smoke in a rain storm."

"Ah, temperance."

George watched his wife, her bobbed hair washed and marcelled for other eyes, her hands, hands which should be his, sorting silver and napkins for strangers, her apron, that starched barrier, rustling as she stepped from buffet to pantry, back and forth, and all the while issuing orders to the hired girl in the kitchen. The middle-aged banker, a little bald, a little stout, sensed his wife's impatience, her wanting to get the table cleared and reset for company, but he continued to sit and watch her, continued to listen to her voice, even knowing that his case was lost.

"It isn't decent, George."

"Who cared decent? You're my wife, this is our home."

It was not a matter of decency, not decency at all, not a question of running a 'Christian' home, not decency, just clothes. "Corset and all," he told himself, "it takes her half an hour to get dressed, and to her one unveiling a day is enough." Like the gentleman that he was he climbed the stairs, alone again for his mid-day nap. "And I suppose today it's the silk stockings…and all six garters. Another time, please, Lord."

Samuel Bunkers was a man also at odds with his wife but for different reasons as the several pairs of feet that appeared daily under his kitchen table attested to the conjugal serenity in his house. Sam's problem was money. He and his wife argued about money, the earning of it and spending of it. Sam had little talent for earning money. His only talent worth notice was that of making whiskey, and in the nineteen twenties this was not a positive attribute, particularly for a man whose wife envied those temperate ladies and their prestigious alliance. Sam farmed two eighties given to him by his father-in-law, but he was always in debt. The small advances he made toward solvency with good crops were usually lost by the arrival of another child. He was in real trouble the day of the LTA meeting at Leadwells. The fifty dollars that he had put aside for his loan payment to the bank had been used to buy sugar and copper tubing, both of which were now hidden in his haymow. Ben Taylor had taken advantage of him, but Sam, nobody's fool, had recognized a better investment of the money, better even than the telephone that his wife wanted, in fact was getting a little stubborn about. And, today, he would somehow have to convince George Leadwell that the bank doors would not close without that fifty dollars.

Amelia White, the full-figured and business-like owner of the town's only hotel, informed the young man standing in her lobby that he would have to find boarding accommodations elsewhere. She had rooms to rent and he was welcome to look at them, but she no longer provided meals.
"You say you are looking for work?"
"Yes, but don't worry, I'll be able to pay. I can pay a week in advance."
"I would like that." His shoes were in good condition and all of his clothes, not new, but good, and the suitcase expensive leather once. She would examine that later. A woman could learn much about a man from his luggage. Now, her probing was casual, "What kind of work are you looking for?"
"I understand that there is a need for hired men on the farms here."
"Farming? You?" Amelia White was a quick judge of men, could spot the flimflam artist or the serious businessman, and she knew that the man standing before her was no farmer. She hid her skepticism with "What I mean to say is that we don't get many transients coming into town by train."
The fabrication, shaped many days earlier, now came easily, "It was just a freight, and the brakeman owed me a favor."

"Stranger in town, up getting a room from Mrs. White. See him, Ralph? Don't think he looks like a hat salesman." George Leadwell was leaning against the brick front of his bank, enjoying the sun and a few visits before starting his afternoon's work. He was talking to Ralph Kellar, the town constable. Ralph had realized long ago that George always enjoyed the sun from the same place, the corner spot with a clear view across the square faced by all of the business places in town and from where he could check the time of day by the whistle of the afternoon freight.

"Oh, I suppose we will find out," Ralph told the man who was responsible for his being hired as the town's chief of police. Ralph was a steady, contented, man. George likes that in a man. Most of his constituents thought of Kellar as a devoted man, devoted to his job and to the memory of his wife, dead some ten years. People are generally sentimental. If George Leadwell suspected a different reason for Kellar's contentment, he did not reveal it. He liked his daily visits with Ralph.

The temperance cabal continued to disrupt George's day. The Reverend Father Farrell snubbed him again, ignored the banker's nod and friendly smile and walked into the town's other bank.

"How can a bunch of women, well taken care of and seemingly sensible women do this?" His voice had been raised but George was always the gentleman. She had been indomitable.

"George, it's against the law!"

"A tiny half cup of wine and you have to make a fuss about it?"

"It's a tiny half cup every day of the week and twice on Sunday!"

"They ain't criminals, Sophia!"

"It's alcohol!"

"But I can't have all the Catholics in town going to the other bank! Don't you understand that?"

The temperance recruit explained to her husband, "We are united in this, George. We are doing our Christian duty. There may be sacrifices. The Lord understands this, why can't you?"

"Onward Christian Soldiers! You're ruining me!"

The bookkeeping troubles had no relation to the LTA. George was a sedate man, at least he understood that people expect dignity and calm from a banker, but a man does have his limits. Warm afternoons were particularly difficult for him with the sun's rays filling his office and stirring up the lingering odor of mothballs in his secretary's sensible dark skirts. On such afternoons George usually kept a cigar going. He was giving serious thought to buying one of those new electric fans that Jap Winters had in his hardware store, brought back with him from his last market trip. An extravagance, but his depositors might look at it as his being progressive.

George was having a problem concentrating on the letter he was dictating. The steps involved in initiating a farm foreclosure were no match for the sight of a trim ankle hosed in lisle. Carnal thoughts. 'Why must she always wear those damned proper shoes? How I would like, just once, to see that instep—and in silk. And, God willing, I'd give a day's wages to that knee'…"Where was I, Leona?"

"The party of the third part, Mr. Leadwell."

His desk was situated so that George could see into the bank's lobby. Even with the door closed he could monitor his financial establishment as the door had a beveled glass top with his name printed on it in small gold and black letters. He saw Sam Bunkers appear at the loan officer's cage and then be shown to a comfortable chair. George interrupted his dictation.

"I see Sam Bunkers waiting to see me. Do you have the papers on his loan application?"

"Yes," the pretty Leona Bloom answered, but did not move to get the needed papers. She cleared her throat.

"Something wrong, Leona?"

"Well, it's not for me to say, and he is new at the job and it really is a new position at the bank, but…"

"Is Percival James stealing from me?"

"No! No, not that. It's just that, that, well he is so nervous and, and a, fluttery. He can't seem to…"

"Well, Leona?"

"He does get his work done…even as slow as he is—I think that comes from being new." Miss Bloom did not feel that it was her place to be critical of another bank employee, but she did manage, "I'm finding mistakes, quite a lot of mistakes."

"What's wrong with him? Is he stupid or something?"

"No. I don't think it's that. He's always been a little high-strung, everybody knows that—you know it yourself. Right now we think it's that baby. It should have been born last week. Of course Julie could have got mixed up." Miss Bloom added hastily, "My mother says that. I don't know things like that." George's secretary was blushing. "All I know is that every time the telephone rings, no matter where he is in the bank, well, it's frightening to see."

George reassured her, "The first one's always the toughest, Leona. Send Bunkers in. Maybe I don't need those papers today."

George Leadwell did not need papers to record money he did not get. He felt obliged, however, to offer Sam some business advice.

"We didn't think that fifty dollars would be too much for you to put together, Sam. We both agreed on that."

"I know it, George. I know that. But a man has to look to the future, and a real good business investment chance came along, and I figured I'd better take advantage of it. Felt you'd agree."

"Anything to do with Ben Taylor?"

It did have to do with Ben Taylor.

"Well, Ben was lucky, got a hold of some information just in time. Seems Ralph Kellar stumbled onto something."

"You should have told me, George."

"Weren't much time, and all I really know is that Ben's going to ease off things for awhile. Strange, I didn't know you had to worry about a hired man."

"You telling me something George?"

"Might be. Thing is now we'll have to get this loan of yours revamped. I'll get the papers, see what we can do."

Miss Bloom had told the truth. The papers were full of mistakes and omissions and scratches and erasures. George Leadwell had a quick mind for figures and had been his own loan officer for years with a minimum of paper work, and he thought that he was a reasonable and understanding employer, but his appearance at the loan officer's cage signaled panic to the young man perched on the high stool. James's voice quivered as he tried to explain the meaning of the figures he had scratched on the heavy sheets of the ledger. His hands shook and his voice got thin and high as he answered each question. Leadwell, who was learning nothing, was at a loss. He tried to calm the young man, but when he had to grab a tipping inkwell, the banker blurted, "Good God, Percy, calm down! Ain't no need for all this!" Bad loans, birthing babies, spilled ink, and a hysterical clerk were too much. George addressed his Maker for the second time that day. "Lord, how'd he ever manage to get that girl pregnant."

"You have a real flair for the brash, George. You knew when you hired the boy that he came from a skittish family!"

"Yes, well…get him home, Ralph. Who'd a thought? Maybe he'll come to before you get him there and maybe, with luck, that baby'll be born tonight, and I'll get my clerk back tomorrow."

"Yeah. But you've got to watch it, George. God knows what you'll say next time."

"Oh, I doubt there'll be a next time, Ralph. Don't think he's got the stomach for it, not for no part of it."

The cleaning for LTA had been thorough. George was accustomed to the regular spring and fall cleaning, each a week long with every corner and every surface in the house laid bare and dusted, scrubbed or painted. But he had been careless, took a chance with this third cleaning, didn't know why anyone would clean the attic for an afternoon of women in his parlor and his dining room.

"When I had Mrs. Adamson here I thought we might as well do it. You're never any help, you know, especially with the lifting."

"Mrs. Adamson lift that trunk?"

"Yes, but I kept it closed, George. I don't give my help excuses to talk about us all over town. And I do think you're unfair with me, especially when I try so hard to be a credit to you." Mrs. Leadwell's face had a pinched, hurt look, "It's not easy being a banker's wife."

"It was medicine, Sophia. Medicine for my lumbago. Your Pa told me it would be good for that."

"You don't have lumbago, George. And I'll thank you not to bring my father into this—you know what a cross his drinking is for my poor mother!" Sophia dabbed delicately at her eyes, faking tears.

"An occasional swig of whiskey? You exaggerate, Sophia. And as to your mother—you brought her up yourself, you know—as far as your mother goes, how about that female medicine she keeps in her pantry?"

This bit of profanity sent Mrs. Leadwell to bed early with a sick headache.

Samuel Bunkers' sheepcote was slowly becoming a reality and, with help from the bank, the new project could develop into a real moneymaker. He had to convince his wife that he should take on the project. She thought that sheep were smelly and a nuisance and wanted no part of the handling of the wool. She expressed doubt that there was a market for the meat and labeled the whole idea, "Another of your hare-brained schemes, Sam." Her father, a successful breeder of cattle, agreed with her, proposed that he take over the management of Sam's land with Sam working for him. He thought it was a wise plan because it pointed to the future, consolidated their efforts and made more production of beef possible. Sam put his foot down as he had the backing of George Leadwell and he distrusted his father-in-law and his two brothers-in-law. He could do this because the land was in his name.

In consideration for his wife, however, Sam put the sheep shelter far from the house, close to the center of the section. He used a strip of grazing land that lay directly behind his hay barn and in the gully of a dry-creek bed. He quieted his wife's objections by explaining to her that the sheep would be far from the house and would be cheaper to feed than cattle.

He started late in February and the work went well as the winter was mild. Taking into account the work he was doing plus the work of spring planting he realized that he would have to have help. Word got around and he hired the first man who applied for the job.

In his own way, Sam Bunkers was a conservative man and a little forward thinking. He saw that the walls of the gully made an excellent wind break, producing a protected place for the young lambs, deep and exposed only to the sun. Sam had little capital but good ideas and one of these was to use the gully walls as part of the cote. There was much digging required with not enough frost in the ground to hamper the shovels, but the softness of the ground caused some cave-ins, consequently, the plans for the shelter were changed frequently.

Sam liked to visit as he worked and enjoyed the company of the man he had hired. Sam called him 'Buzz' as he was not sure of his real name, in fact had not questioned the man very closely, figured he was qualified for the work as it takes little talent for a man to shovel or push a wheelbarrow. But the young fellow was pleasant, his kids liked him and Sam's wife even fixed up a bed for him in an old tool shed, over-fed him as she did with everybody.

Buzz took an interest in the work. It was he who discovered the high water markings in the bank of the gully, suggested that a good rain might cause the whole project to collapse if they dug deeper. The shelter was fashioned like a cave. Sam planned to hang a tarp over the opening and build some stalls or benches on the inside wall. With the discovery of the water markings they realized that the roof would have to be higher and probably thinner. Sam was no engineer, but he was a gambler as most farmers must be. He thought a prop or two would be sufficient. He was wrong again. After three weeks of digging and shaping they went to work one morning to find the roof collapsed on to the floor of the cave. Sam realized that he would have to have more capital.

"If I have to roof that thing over it will take some money," he told his banker. "I'll have to buy something to cover it."

"Well, yes, I understand that." George Leadwell was thinking that he might have made a mistake, that he should have listened to Sam's father-in-law. But he had got this far and Sam's project could be a providential investment.

"I hear you hired help. He any good?"
"He can shovel and he can lift."
"He know anything about sheep?"
"Don't think so. Not so far, I'd say."

The banker nodded. He, too, was an ingenious man, knew where Sam could get the material he needed at a better than fair price. Sam drove home with a wagonload of old thin roofing and several charred timbers from the town's latest fire.

Buzz argued against the backbreaking chore of saving the sod from the roof, but Sam insisted that they cut and roll it so that after the tin was installed they could cover it with sod.

"What in hell for, Sam? We can make that roof leak-proof at least as leak-proof as you need it for a few days of lambing."

"Well, you see it's this way, Buzz. It's for Mrs. Bunkers. She works hard to keep things looking nice and one of her arguments against this business was that I was just making another eyesore. So to please her, I figure we can keep it looking like a hill."

"An eyesore out here in the middle of the field an eyesore you can't even see from the house?"

"I know. But the sun could catch the roof, like a signal or something. My wife wouldn't like that, not at all. If you were married, which you ain't, you'd know that women think funny."

Two young men, both new to the community, were playing pool in the musty back section of the town's remaining saloon. It was not a saloon in the strictest sense of the word with prohibition rampant in the land, but the owner managed to survive as a businessman by selling tobacco, soda pop, and near beer. His place was something of an old man's club with the non-working seniors of the town gathering there for euchre and pitch. In warm weather they spent part of their days sitting and visiting in the sun along storefronts. Most stores had wide steps for sitting as they had been built before paved streets came into being. Businessmen had wanted their floors to be as high as they could be above the mud and manure of what was called Main Street. In cold weather, if these oldsters were not playing cards they were gathered around the pot-bellied stove at JP Winter's hardware store. Their number varied. If a new man came along they could always find a nail keg for him to sit on—first comers got the chairs, a ramshackle collection of rejects from kitchens and church basements in the community. These seniors were generally experts on the lies told by politicians and the town's two newspapers. Gentlemen to the core, they did not speculate on or pry into the business of the two men playing pool. They all remembered being young.

Well trained in discretion and double-talk the pool players made their plans under cover of "Two bits says I can put the five in the side pocket." They also watched the front door carefully and could identify every man in the saloon.

The older, slicker-looking man of the two, muttered carefully, "He thinks I'm taken in by that vat of beer in the basement—let me find it. How dumb does he think I am? He spends his time 'cleaning' the barn, sends me out to fix fence. I've damned near fixed a mile of fence."

"You ain't found the stuff yet?"

"I thought sure it was in the grain room, and still think it's there. I've thrown a pitchfork in there a dozen times, but I've yet to hit glass."

"What'll you do?"

"I don't have to find it. We just have to catch him moving it. They want the pole at the other end. Word is, it will be soon."

"What am I supposed to do?"

"Hear you're in the sheep business."

"Go to hell. My arms and back are damned near ruined."

"Stick it out. I need you close. Do you think anyone suspects anything?"

"Thought that woman at the hotel was nosier than she needed to be."

"Ah. Mrs. White."

Ben Taylor's hired man enlisted the help of Ralph Kellar. In response to the constable's statement that he was 'busy enough keeping the town clean, don't need to poke into county affairs', the federal agent explained that he had the power to deputize Kellar and could make it difficult for him to be reappointed to his job if he did not cooperate. Ralph understood this. He had great respect for the ministerial association and, in particular, for John Barton, an elder in the Methodist church, and an avid prohibitionist. So Ralph agreed to be deputized and was told by George Leadwell that he had made a good decision.

In that conversation George confided to Ralph that the Senator was coming to town in the near future, on one of his annual campaign swings through the area. George wanted everything in the community to be shipshape for this honored visit.

"Staying at your place again, George?"

"I plan it that way, Ralph, although currently there is a problem."

"He could stay at Mrs. White's."

"Yes, and I do appreciate that dear lady's contribution to this community, but, thank you, no. NO."

"I suppose she don't have any fancy lady bedspreads." The policeman looked quickly at the banker, gauging his tolerance for fun, then added, "He did take his boots off, George. I'd say that's pretty good for an old cowboy."

"Ralph, I don't need that from you. Mrs. Leadwell is quite enough, besides, the problem is more serious than our best bedspread."

"Oh, that problem. Well, busy times ahead."

The plan was set. Ben Taylor had driven the appointed route three times, his destination a seemingly abandoned barn just across the state line, a distance of about ten miles from Ben's farm and through flat, low-lying fields and a range of low hills. The road was rough, parts of it not graveled and some of it only one lane. The road was not much of a trick for a well-trained team, but Ben wanted to test it for his truck. He was a careful man, left little to chance. He had chosen the night of the Elks spring dance, believing that all of the law enforcement officers would be occupied by this big social event. If his wife insisted on going to the dance she could get a ride with the Bunkers.

Ben had dismantled his still when Ralph Kellar, alerted by the man's extravagance, had had the local telephone operator listen in on one of his hired man's telephone calls. Ben hated that he had had to take advantage of Sam, but there were just so many places on one farm that a man could hide things. He would make it up to Sam, who knew that no one fooled with Leavenworth. Ben left nothing to chance and worked alone. He figured that one man could lift and load the jugs of whiskey in an hour's time, and he knew the road, knew he could drive it at night easily. Ralph Kellar would be working the dance, as every young blood in the area would be there with enough hip flasks to keep the law busy. Ben had fired his hired man, got him off the place. Everything was set.

The Bunkers' hired man, Buzz, could not be persuaded to go to the dance. The children pleaded with him, and Mrs. Bunkers reminded him of all of the pretty young girls who would be there, the good food in the box lunches that would be auctioned; but he blushed, said he didn't know how to dance and was always tripping all over himself around girls, so Sam's truck went down the road without him, but loaded with all of the Bunkers and Mrs. Ben Taylor and her two.

Federal agent, John Longman, the Taylor's recently discharged hired man, had also driven the route that Ben Taylor studied so carefully, had also made plans and felt sure of success. He had spied on Taylor, heard him make that long distance call, knew that the whiskey would be moved that night. When Ralph Kellar flatly refused to help him, citing the dance as his excuse, Longman decided that he and the Shepherd could make the raid alone. He stationed himself in his hideout, a copse of trees near the Taylor farm, where he was certain to see any move made by Taylor. He planned to give the farmer a head start, pick up the Shepherd, and the two of them would follow the bootlegger from a safe distance, follow him across the state line and to the old barn where Ben would make his sale. Two other agents were hidden near the barn and would help with the arrest. Crossing the state line made the sale a federal offense. The erstwhile farmhand liked his work, thought of himself as an espionage specialist. When he made plans with the Shepherd he called himself 'The Fox' and Ben Taylor 'The Rabbit'.

All went according to plan. The Rabbit's truck, parked for so long near the barn, left the yard and started down the road, its light dim in the dark night. The Shepherd was waiting near the Bunkers' farm and the two agents, very alert, were able to position their car about a quarter of a mile behind the Taylor truck as it chugged down the road. The Rabbit drove slowly. The two young men were impatient but knew that the farmer/bootlegger could not risk bumps or false turns with his cargo. The Fox was exultant, tired of his stint in this slow backcountry and looking forward to a new assignment, possibly a promotion after tonight's haul. Both men discussed future plans. The Shepherd admitted that he liked the Bunkers, even liked this part of the country, and mentioned an interest in the 'looker' who worked at the bank. At times in the hills they lost sight of the Taylor truck but would find it again after a turn in the road. They were jubilant, knew that they were nearing the state line when the road flattened. The Fox now drove faster, wanting to be closer to the Rabbit when he crossed the state line. He had checked the road carefully, but he was sort of a greenhorn about the weather in the area, did not know how quickly a roadbed can change when deprived of frost. In his previous trips he had easily driven through the frozen rust, but a couple of days of March sun had turned a low spot in the road into a mud hole. Everything the two men tried to do with the car just made it sink deeper into the muck. Swearing, spinning, and pushing the wheels just worsened their predicament. When the beam of a flashlight showed the rear tires in mud up to their hub caps, the Fox ordered the Shepherd to walk, to get down the road as fast as he could.

"Those guys are waiting. They'll get Taylor. Have them come back and help me get this damned car out."

A half-mile down the road, the Shepherd found the Rabbit parked and waiting. Ben managed to turn his truck around in the narrow road and they went back to get the Fox. All the Rabbit said was, "You guys have to learn that when that road gets squishy you hit the shoulders or as much of the dry weeds as you can."

There was no whiskey in Ben's truck. Never had been any.

Back in town Ben Taylor had time for two dances with his wife after which he took his family home.

The two agents spent the night in jail, the Fox on a 'drunk and disorderly' charge and the Shepherd there because Ralph Kellar said he needed help and deputized him.

Sam Bunkers danced the first two dances with his wife. She always got sore feet after two dances and then he could do as he pleased. He found that Ben Taylor was right. One man could load the whiskey in less than an hour. And he, Sam, was right—that sheepcote was just big enough to hold Ben's whiskey and all that remained of Ben's still.

Buzz decided there was a real future in banking.

The Fox spent three days in jail. He could have gone free after one night, but he added 'intimidation of a police officer' to his charges. Ralph Kellar did his duty; he investigated the case thoroughly.

"That was my best gin, Ralph!"

"We appreciate that." The constable hesitated, searching for the right words, a matter of fidelity. He spoke slowly with a bit of emphasis, "We did not mean for you, to, ah, that is, to *completely* demoralize that man of Ben's."

The hotel matron understood his problem, "Well, what happened, Ralph, is that when I took my corset off, his legs just seemed to buckle."

"I believe that."

"Of course he'd had three of my lemonades."

"I understand, Amelia. I understand completely."

"I thought you would, Ralph. Why don't you pull up that quilt? It gets cold in these back rooms."

Epilogue

Joseph Campbell summarizes Jane Goodall's observations about apes thus:

The male is not engaged, like the female, in the constant charge of children. He has a lot of time. He knows where the bananas are, but it isn't time to go there now, and nobody's bothering us, so what do we do? This is it, in men's clubs, delousing each other…a long-standing institution.

A Girl on a Bus

"My God, Mother, not the bus! You don't know what you'll run into, the people, the riff-raff you…"

"Look, I can leave from and return to my own main street where my car will be parked, waiting for me. Besides, do you know it costs me at least twenty-five dollars for a taxi from the airport to Jane's house? And then I have to sit there all afternoon waiting for her."

The argument goes on, hers, a fake skirmish, her insurance, her show of 'responsibility for Mother', a demonstration for later reporting, "I told her not to take the bus, but you know how damned stubborn she can be!" And the others, my others, will agree and thus absolve her of any blame in case there's an accident,…maybe a theft, a mugging, a rape. A rape? Hah! More likely, a stroke.

I ride the bus because it makes sense to me, and because traveling thus I have a precious span of time in which I can be frivolous, alone, anonymous, free to daydream, to wander through the days of my life, perhaps again see the face of an old love, and pretend his nearness, perhaps again relish old victories or sensibly write-off old failures. Alone on a bus, I can speak or be silent. And I can act unencumbered by remonstrations from those who love me.

The passengers on my buses are mostly just different versions of me, grandmothers on a trip to see grandchildren, shop, and maybe see a movie. On our buses, you see a lot of shopping bags, all stuffed with handwork, afghans, pillows. You can smell oranges and salad dressing. Occasionally, there is a man sitting among us. He is usually well dressed, clean, dignified, and talks only to the bus driver. He carries loneliness with him.

Older couples are a rarity on our buses. Those of my crowd, who still have each other, ride through the country in RVs or made-over pickups. They explore the tourist traps, often-dressed alike—same windbreaker, same colored slacks. They wear T-shirts and sweat shirts decorated with slogans from the tourist industry. You find them in those highway places, together selecting new souvenirs.

I don't ride the buses for talk. I've had enough of who's cousin lives in my town, what the weather is doing to the crops, and all of those dramatic tales about encounters with the medical profession. I have become an expert at looking unapproachable. That is, until the driver announces something like the fact that he is turning around and going back to Minneapolis because of the current blizzard. Then, I talk. I want to know everything. And I, like everyone else on the bus, wonder where I will be spending the night, wondering also if I can escape somebody else's idiotic decision. I now know that I should have taken that jet, but I brazenly join the clucking of the other passengers, their buzz of worry about when we will get home, and how. Among us is a woman in her eighties, thin and frail, her clothes layered on, a sweater under her long coat, a ragged scarf, some knitted thing on her head with strands of gray hair framing her face. We also see bare, frosty white ankles above worn oxfords.

The woman across the aisle from me knows about her, tells me that she lives in a nursing home near Collegeville. "I wonder how she got to the Twin Cities dressed like that. The nursing home people would never have let her out without something more on her feet. She must have snuck out on them."

"Could be." A knowledgeable descendant of a woman who kept running away from home the last five years of her life, I ask, "What will they do with her in Minneapolis?"

"Oh, the bus company will put her in a hotel for the night. They will do that for all of us." She continued, "Don't worry about the old woman, she has money. She owned one of those buildings they tore down in Bloomington."

Money! I ask, "Do you believe that?"

"Oh, sure. She's smart, used to be a high school teacher. She'll get back to Collegeville all right."

A former high school teacher and still fighting her own battles at eighty? This old lady with bare ankles gives me courage, a courage I imitated on my next trip home when I decide that I must engage in a protest against the bus company.

My town is off their list, my town that they always drove through on their way to Thunder Flats. I felt that they needed to know that they had made a mistake, that one simple turn would get them to where I wanted to go, where they had gone for years and with a second turn they'd be back on the road to Thunder Flats.

A confused clerk at the ticket counter in Minneapolis was my unwitting ally, sold me a ticket to my town. She told me that I would arrive at midnight, but I pretended not to hear her.

The driver discovered the mistake just before we left Minneapolis. He tried to explain to me what I would have to do and that I should call my family when we stopped in Thunder Falls. His bus was loaded with refugees from snow-packed highways so he was too preoccupied to suspect my deceit. I knew that no insurance company in the world would permit him to leave any old lady alone on any highway in the country.

In my defense, you should know that he made a mistake about the term 'Junction'. He used the word as it is used in his route book. I use the right meaning, the local meaning, of the word. There is only one real 'Junction' between Thunder Falls and Thunder Flats.

I discovered his mistake when he turned at my Junction and did not sop. I could see my son standing there waiting for me, as I had asked him to do. I tried to explain this to the driver during the eight miles to his next stop, but he was stubborn, would not admit he was wrong. The argument continued on the returning eight miles back to the Junction, and he was gaining support from the other passengers. Only a few of them were on the bus in Minneapolis when he told me what I should do, but he talked louder than I could, and of course none of them dared to be on my side.

I was becoming desperate and when we were again approaching my Junction I said in a loud voice, "I am going to report you to your superiors!" It was my school-teacher voice, the one that teachers learn early in their careers, a trick of throwing their voices so that no kid, not even one in the back row can get by with the excuse that he didn't hear you. I've used it all my life because it works in family life too. It's a voice that is a little threatening, is meant to be threatening.

When I saw my son for the second time that night, I called out, "There's my son waiting!"

The driver stopped the bus, quickly found my bags and then rushed over to my son, and stood there shouting at him and waving his arms, with me and all of the other passengers watching. My son, who is a lawyer, did not move or speak until we were in his car. Then I heard, "What in hell was that all about?"

"That driver? He's a poor loser."

The only people I remember seeing on any of my buses who would be described as riff-raff were three young people, a girl and two boys, all of them dressed pretty tacky, tacky like they didn't have much money, not tacky like it's the style now. They looked to be younger than twenty. It was one of those cloudy, dark December days and they found seats in the back, the darkest part of the bus. Just as we expected, the bus driver had to tell them that they could not smoke on the bus, and that if they wanted to listen to their music, they'd have to use earphones.

One wonders, what does a sixteen-year old girl do with two boys in the dark of a bus? Maybe the second boy because her father told her she could not be alone with the first boy. Or maybe the second boy because the first boy was scared and needed some kind of moral support. She would be his girl.

If you've ever been that third party, like the second boy, you quickly realize that no one is scared anymore, and you wish to God that you'd stayed home.

I don't worry about that girl in the back of the bus because I have learned that in the wink of an eye she will be buying C or D cups and will have moved from the Petite to the Large section at Dayton's.

On the trip home, the twenty-four-hour-late-because-of-the-blizzard trip, a D-cup got on the bus at the town of the Green Giants. She had stayed there the night because she did not want to ride back to Minneapolis and stay in a downtown hotel.

Because of her and a book I read, I began to think differently about the Giant's town. Up until then, I thought of it only as part of what must be one of the most beautiful places in the world, the valley of the Minnesota River, a place that, so far, no one has been able to spoil. There are many roads here, one of them a major interstate highway, but the road builders seem to have hidden these new trails well, tucked them in like ridges or braces at the bottoms of the hills with nothing slashing through the flames of color on the tree-laden slopes in autumn or staining the whiteness of the snow that surrounds the pines in winter.

If I were to go back to that town of giants, I would go as a tourist, and I would go to the Mayo house but not to see the home of a famous man. I would go to walk in the yard of that house. I would step in the place where Mrs. Mayo and most of the other women of this prairie town marched. They marched to fool an enemy who would attack a town devoid of its men, men gone to fight a war.

The Indians of the area had gone on the warpath, fighting the U.S. Government, who in the wisdom of some hapless clerk, had cut the food rations for the tribe. Dr. Mayo and the men of the community had become Uncle Sam's army. Mrs. Mayo had joined the other army wives who had donned their husband's clothes, covered their braids with men's caps, and with a hose or a rave over their shoulders, marched up and down the settlement. They looked like bona fide soldiers to the enemies who were watching from across the valley.

I would walk in the yard of a genuine heroine.

There is a dark side to this story, dark but also wonderful, depending on your point of view. That Indian war was short-lived and when it ended, everything was tidied up, the dead buried where they had fallen. Later, some of the bodies were dug up by the few medical people in the area. Actually, it was body snatching for the study of anatomy. Such activities took place in the dark of night and were not publicized. It's my own idea, but I would look at the Mayo house and think that that basement had to have held some of that study material. I believe that Charley and Will's mother would have permitted that.

On the bus with the teen-age trio there was another D-cup across the aisle from me. By chance, in the fading light, I saw a tear on her cheek. Lucky for me, because I heard a wonderful story. She was going home, back to her home in the upper prairies of South Dakota. She was going to that farmhouse for the first time alone. That's what death does. It makes what once was a home into a scary, empty place, especially at night when, before death, the night was a time of a life-long embrace.

"You've never been alone on your farm?" I ask.

"Oh, yes, I was alone there for several months after my husband died."

"Are you worried about your farm, can you, or do you want to manage it by yourself?" I justify my curiosity, "I would be frightened. My husband always attended to the business."

"No. I can manage the farm. I just don't like coming home alone."

"Where have you been?" I ask this, but I already pegged her as one with grandchildren in the Twin Cities.

"Mexico."

Then I heard the story of their son who, as a student at State College, studied Engineering, Electrical Engineering, and he must have done well because he was hired by a large firm. He earned a series of promotions and at present, was part of a project on the Acapulco side of Mexico. His company had expanded, built a plant there, plus a planned city for its employees. My companion described a beautiful city and a wonderful opportunity for the people of Mexico.

I asked if she would consider moving there.

"Not right now. I have the farm and like living there. We talked of my living with him and his family, but he is due for another promotion soon, and may move back to this country. We'll see then."

I was remembering my own nights of coming home to an empty house. Sunday nights were the worst. My youngest daughter would spend her weekends with me, and I would drive her back to college Sunday nights. I told my new friend about this.

"You know, I was lucky. By some fortunate chance, the Perry Mason show was rerun at ten o'clock on Sunday night. That meant that I could come home to watch and listen to old friends, people I knew well, trustworthy people cleaning out the corners of evil in our lives."

Encouraged by her silence, I continued, "Find something that you want to come home to, maybe a quilt frame, a canvas and paints, a typewriter, something you always wanted to do and never took time for."

She was no longer crying, was, in fact, laughing a little, this engineer's mother laughing at a silly woman and her silly ideas. I ventured more.

"And buy yourself a new night gown. Be sure to get something really soft and silky, something that feels good next to your skin. It is time to reward yourself."

On one trip, a March-cold day, we waited longer than the usual twenty minutes at Mankato. We were told that we were waiting for a bus coming from a Hutterite colony in the area. The idea of a distinctive, different-acting group of people descending on you is somewhat unsettling. You scrunch up your shoulders and stare at the window or at a book in your lap, hoping to discourage any one of them from taking the empty seat next to you.

I have nothing against Hutterites, other than what I consider to be their odd ideas about progress. My experience with them is limited. The first time I talked to a Hutterite was at a private girls' school where I was teaching. I was in the principal's office because I had been asked to substitute for her while she was out of town. I looked up once and saw a man staring at me. I had not heard him come. He was tall and slender, had black hair, a full beard and was wearing a black hat with a wide brim. I don't know which of us was the more frightened. Luckily, I remember that the school occasionally bought food from a nearby Hutterite colony, and he managed to say, 'melons'. I directed him to the kitchen where he could deal with the cook. She had been at the school much longer than I.

That same fall, with some of our students, I drove out to the colony. I remember only some gray buildings and a muddy farmyard. We were intruders.

With my marriage, I gained a sister-in-law who was a county superintendent of schools. This was long before the days of consolidation, and she had jurisdiction over a school at a Hutterite colony. She found these people to be cooperative and sincere about their children's education. She never talked to a mother, which in fact, of course, confirmed my suspicions that Hutterite women were voiceless. How interesting bias is, as I must confess that in my own town, the town where I raised my family, no woman gained a seat on the school board, the city council, or the country club board until the late eighties. My sister-in-law has been dead for a quarter of a century.

I frequently accompanied my husband to the conventions he attended. One spring, in a town in a central part of the state, I found a wholesale yard goods store. I was always in the market for new sewing ideas and for bargains. One time, I was surprised to find several Hutterite women shopping near me, all dressed very much alike, a long dark skirt protected by a cotton length apron, a light triangular scarf over a dark blouse with elbow-length sleeves. Each wore a cotton cap to cover her hair, even the youngest of girls with them. They seemed to be enjoying their outing and enjoying each other as they talked and laughed together. I ached to talk to one of them, tried not to stare, but they easily ignored me, gave no indication of seeing me. I learned later that they traded goose feathers and other home made products for bolts of material. They bought yards of huck toweling.

My sensitive nose detected a body odor when they were near me, the full warm smell of working people. What a privilege they had, freedom to live without the constant need to deodorize oneself!

In the many years since that encounter, I have learned that Hutterite colonies are wealthy and that their men are expert farmers.

Six adults and three children boarded my bus, all of them in black or dark gray clothes, the four women in a sort of suit, trim and flattering, with a long skirt and long sleeves. The two men and the boy wore identical dark suits and those remarkable wide-brimmed hats, even one on the boy who could not have been more than three or four years old.

I tried to behave, but I was bursting with curiosity. I strained to hear their talk as they chatted and laughed among themselves. They were not speaking English. I was hearing what I have been told is a dialect of old German.

So, I satisfied myself with sneak looks at the woman in front of me, the mother of two of the children, and at the woman across the aisle from me, a very new mother. One does not stare at a woman nursing her child, but I was able, with quick looks, to discover that the buttons on her suit front were part of a clever pattern that allowed her to nourish her child with dignity and privacy.

The shoulder line of the suit ahead of me was hand sewn as was the white lace cap that covered her hair, and from what I could see of her husband's coat.

I guessed that this party of colonists was on their way to a new home. I guessed also that the two young women with them were unmarried and were on their way to meet husbands-to-be in the new colony. As we were leaving the bus, I asked the woman in front of me where they were going. She answered me in very good English.

Our route took us through the farm country of southern Minnesota, the cradle of an international grain dynasty. The abundance, the potential of the area, seemed to be on the young father's mind, as during the trip, he would hold his son up to the window and say words like 'cattle' and 'tractor'. Perhaps what he saw from the window helped to ease the sorrow he must have felt when taking his family away from grandparents, brothers and sisters, away from people he would seldom see in his new life.

My last sight of this company of pioneers was in the bus terminal at Thunder Falls, the women now wearing black bonnets and long graceful capes. Standing among the rest of us, we in oversized athletic shoes, lumpy slacks and cheaply decorated T-shirts and jackets, these colonists looked almost regal, a sovereignty in their poise, and in their approach to life.

What I remember most clearly, however, is a young male face; I think a face free of acne only shortly before fatherhood. The two young men had left the bus at one of its stops on its way west. This man returned to hand his wife a role of Life Savers. I saw joy in his face, joy and adoration.

I suspect that my trio in the back of the bus tell themselves that they are going to California, possibly Arizona, but I believe that they will go no farther than Omaha. There is work there and people easy to know, and the girl hedging her bets with the knowledge that home is just a bus ride away. I wish that girl well, enough victories, a life as productive as those of her sisters on the bus, and now and then the tremor of a lover's fingers as he places a gift in her hand.

Crucify!

They came from all directions, but mostly from the East and from the North, came to this southern place with its space, its winds and desert, came to a comfortable place, humbler than the cities of their own livelihoods and thus a place for grief unencumbered by any need to show or defend their own worthiness, their own slowly earned prosperity.

Many of them rode together, sharing cars to save gas money. Only those held by jobs or some such obligation drove alone, and they came late, their arrivals signaling more tears, everyone's sorrow erupting anew. The latecomers missed the first family rosary, but some choked down sandwiches and hot coffee and sobbed while the prayers were called out.

Maryann and Martin arrived first. She was the oldest sister and was needed now that there was no mother. She had brought extra quilts and food, and some saved dark clothes for the children who must be dressed solemnly for the mass. She would begin an endless round of ironing shortly after she arrived, and she would manage the house, all of the women gauging their activities by what they believed Maryann wanted.

Hank and Edith rode with Martin and Maryann as Martin's touring car, even second-hand and old, was more splendid looking than Hank's sedan. Hank sat in the back seat with Edith, squeezing her hands under the car quilt to let Martin drive as fast as he wanted. Edith never relaxed, could tell when the speedometer crept past forty and would speak out if Hank were not there to silence her. They had a five-hour drive and hoped to arrive before sundown. Night driving was scary. A box in the seat between Maryann and Martin held carefully wrapped sandwiches and cookies and a thermos of coffee. The women said it was senseless to spend money for food on the road, especially with prices so high and you not knowing the people you were dealing with. Highway robbery.

Hank, terribly upset because he had loved his sister-in-law, spluttered one time, "I told him, told him when I was there last summer, that he had to get that road fixed! That turn before the bridge has always been too sharp, but no, he'd have to spend some money. Just asking for an accident!"

Maryann said nothing, nor did Martin speak, but of course, he was only a brother-in-law, besides, all three of them knew that Hank would not say it again. And they understood why he had to say it once.

They never did see Jacob cry. When they arrived, the house was full of people, neighbors and friends, beginning the wake. All talked in undertones, the men agreeing that women were not meant to drive a car, not having the strength or the mechanical know-how, and women speculating about, "Who he will get, the children need a woman." Jacob scarcely noticed his family's arrival. He was giddy with strain, talking too much, not daring to stop talking. Not daring to test himself with his own silence, test his control over those inner steel-like bands of a merciful shock that kept him from a complete and perhaps idiotic collapse. He talked, babbled, did not stop when he saw Maryann, just talked more, introduced his family to the neighbors, talked with a voice hoarse from strain.

No one rested the second day, the women busy with the house, so many calls, offers of help and so much food, women at the back door with, "Just a little to tide you over." The children were brought home from the houses of friends. Each had been taken by a different mother, diverted from the awful loneliness looming over them, the loneliness they would carry with them always. The reality of death was parceled out stingily to those who were hurt the most. At home, the children looked soberly at relatives, felt the change, escaped to their own rooms only to discover that that space, too, had been invaded by strangers, their clothes and their suitcases. The older children were the most puzzled by it all, and the most frightened. The two youngest were carried about all day, never allowed to cry.

The official investigation of the accident began the second morning. With so many cars coming and going, measurements must be made at once, skid marks traced, the wreckage pulled out from under the bridge. She had been thrown clear of the car. Mercy of God.

Martin and Hank stayed with Jacob through it all, saying little, but missing nothing, facing ugly reality at Jacob's side. Martin talked hardly at all. What he believed or saw, no one would ever know. To him, blame, justice, guilt, were within the jurisdiction of God, and Him alone, superior to man's earth-bound judgments. Martin believed that a man's salvation was defined by his obedience to divine purpose. He had only to look at Jacob to see the hand of God already at work.

Hank, with less faith in God's mercy, struggled with a different truth. The force, the spirit of love that had made him and made his brother was threatening what he had learned and what he had done for himself. Ashamed of his inner war, at once hating and loving an older brother, he stood at the side of the man who had always had what he wanted or had been able to take, the only one of them with cash, while the rest were straddled with payments, the brother of conquests now doomed to sleep alone.

The two men, brother and brother-in-law, stayed with Jacob through the day. They listened to questions from the police—how well did she drive, where was she going, could she have been hurrying, were the tires old, faulty, the brakes—and they followed him to the parish house and to the mortuary and stood with him while he was told by a physician how his wife had died, what blow had killed her.

He knew that he must stop her talk. If only her father or the old priest were still here they would tell her that she was wrong, could tell her, she would listen to them. They could tell her that she should not say what she was saying, that what she was doing could be sinful. If she continued she might make herself sick, but to himself, he wondered if she might be right. He argued.

"You have had her dead since she went out there. Year after year, you worry, the cold, the isolation, always something. You have had her dead with pneumonia the last five winters, and if it wasn't that, it was something else, thieves, wild animals. You forget that she was happy enough to go there with him."

"I don't forget that, but he never told her when he asked her to marry him that she would have to go so far from us! Ask Etta, we talked about it this morning!"

"Etta? She's a fine one to listen to, only married Cliff when she saw that she saw couldn't have Jacob herself."

"What a terrible thing to say! You have always hated my family!" She was sobbing.

"I only hate the way they twist the truth, the way you're doing now. Come, don't cry so. You know he loved her, and you know that she loved him, would have gone any place with him."

"But she was a good driver! Could drive before any of us!"

"Yes,...I know...we will learn what happened, but you must stop this talk. It will lead to quarreling and bitterness, and you don't want that for the last time we will be with her. Besides that, you are making yourself miserable."

He feared that the bad talk was only starting and wished that he had not asked Etta and Cliff to ride with them, such a long ride and Etta always bursting with talk. And he worried about Cliff, whose attempts to control his wife's bad temper usually ended in embarrassment for everyone, as she would lash out at her husband, belittling him. Others in the family pitied Cliff, but they knew that he could stop her talk and would when he chose to. No one in her own family had ever dared to try that. On this trip, he stopped her criticism of Jacob.

"Yes, she had it hard with so much work, six children, and not so much to work with as you. Remember that she could have complained, but she didn't. She could have asked for more. Are you saying that he denied her? Ever? And remember that her children, your nieces and nephews, will be wealthy. None of the rest of us will ever come close to that."

During the funeral mass, Jacob talked to God. He always talked to God during a mass, could carry on a conversation with Him without missing any of the responses. His children were proud of his deep voice and the way that he could remember the strange Latin words. He never talked to God during the rosary. The nuns who had taught him when he was a boy had pointed to the statue of the Blessed Virgin Mary and him to think about Her while the rosary was prayed, so all of his life, whenever he heard the words 'Hail Mary' he saw a beautiful woman dressed in blue and white looking down to him with a loving smile. She kept him good. He loved the sound of the words 'Holy Mary, Mother of God'.

His talks with God were not prayer words, or such words as might be thought of as love. They were reports of a sort, a continuing examination of conscience, a constant search for approval from a stern authority.

Jacob was uncomfortable with, and a little skeptical about, his ability to make money. Driven by the poverty of his childhood, he had sought the security of wealth, only to be surprised by his successes, surprised and humbled by them. Shaped by his early life, he saw money as a grave responsibility and himself a mere caretaker of that money while he was on Earth, a short time indeed when compared to an eternity with God. His family and his church reinforced that belief. They all knew that extravagance with money was sinful, a sin of pride.

Jacob's discussions with God were always respectful, but frequently, they were demanding. He looked for, expected guidance. He was confused when he talked to God during his wife's funeral mass. Agonized, he would look at the casket, the box for her bruised and broken body, and then he would look at the monstrance and ask God why He had let this terrible thing happen.

"How could you do this to me and to my children? Penance? Hah! This is not Penance, this is more like what You let happen to Your own son…for penance, You make me prosperous, then You take my money, take it freely. A new roof for the church. Schoolbooks. And all the while keeping me on my knees, telling me that the new house, the new road, can wait, and then You use the old road so shamefully…You are a selfish God, taking her…I give and yet You take more…I babble, babble like a child, forgive me, forgive my sins, help me to see them…"

❦   ❦   ❦

Hank, sleepless in his brother's house, had left his bed before dawn only to find Jacob alone in the kitchen, the table at which he sat littered with the remains of the night's agony. Hank shook the grate of the range, added kindling to the ashes burning so low, then turned to Jacob. "How long have you been here? I'd say all night from the looks of the cigarette butts and the coffee cups."

"Yes, it's been all night. I can't sleep."

"Making yourself sick won't help. You have to take care of yourself. And you're going to have to slow down, quit this damned working all the time."

Jacob's hand shook as he lit another cigarette.

"You've lived on nothing but cigarettes and coffee for three days now, and I suppose three nights. Am I right?"

Jacob did not answer, seemed not to have heard, and began talking of other things.

"When Ma died it was awful, but she was old, had been so sick, and we had to take care of her for so long. We did what we could. You were the youngest and maybe you don't remember, but the rest of us took turns with her, and when she died, we were ready for it, had done what we could accepted her death."

Hank, afraid of what he might hear, afraid to look at his brother, stood at a window watching the dawn, trying to keep his eyes, his mind, on the day that was beginning, but Jacob's voice continued, his voice and his misery filling the room.

"Why I can't sleep, what I keep hearing is that son-of-a-bitch sheriff questioning me about the car when it was his brother, his own brother, the mechanic, who was at fault. He stole from me, overcharged me again and again, and most of the time, didn't even do the work. I decided not to let him do that again, even if I had to take the car out of town. Don't you see that if only he had been decent, it might not have happened…but then, maybe I shouldn't say that when I don't know for sure what did happen."

Jacob joined Hank at the window, watched the fiery sky as it turned yellow, "What bothers me, what really bothers me, what goes over and over in my mind is that I am not sure that I warned about those brakes. I think I told her—I have to believe that, Hank—but I don't remember for sure. If I knew for sure that I told her, maybe I could relax a little, maybe accept her death better."

Hank said nothing.

Jacob spoke again, "I can tell you this, but just you. I cannot tell her family…they would never forgive me…nor would my children."

On their way home, a tire ruptured, causing Martin's car to careen into the ditch. No one was hurt, but they all were terribly frightened.

Martin blamed himself, "I knew that that was weak, should have got a new one."

His own self-respect, the core of his being, never threatened by his brother-in-law, Hank quickly reassured him, "It was an accident, not your fault."

Edith said, "It never rains, but when it does, it pours…we'll have to be extra careful now. You know these things come in threes."

Emma's Lament

An Excerpt from <u>Castrato</u>

"And where's his holiness gone this time?"

The pungent green tea steamed from the cup as she sipped it quickly, greedily, her tired old body craving its heat. Only when the scalding brew had warmed her through did she put the cup down and pick up a dry hard clump, a 'vanilly' drop cookie, and immerse it in the tea, immerse it to release its sweetness in her mouth. The soft pulp no threat to her chipped and yellowed teeth.

"A new project. It has taken him south." Emma O'Meara watched her sister thoughtfully, her own tea cooling in a china saucer. She hesitated, was in no mood to argue this morning, but she did say, "He has a name."

"He'll never change."

'How safe she is,' thought Emma, 'still safe from the old ones, the old ones who never, never neglected family, never let go, never put them out, instead housed them, fed them, lived with them, lived with their needs, their bad tempers, their 'in-sickness-and-in-health', to keep them safe, safe form an evil and harmful world. Emma parried, "Celia Wilkin's mother likes that new home real well, has a room of her own."

"Glorified funeral parlor."

Emma retaliated, "They're not so bad for them as can afford it. And Celia herself is no spring chicken."

The older woman ignored the argument and its barb, "I'm not going and I know you won't send me. We both know you can squeeze more out of my social security than any of them can." She reminded her sister, "And there's the china, and my silver. And the Honda."

"Those bonds won't even bury you today."

"So put me in a pauper's grave. And you can have the plot next to my Will. You always did want him, and dead you can have him." She waited, sipping her tea, then teased, "You'd miss me."

A light laugh, "You old hellion, still picking on Will and him dead, what is it, twenty years? I never did want him. I just wanted you to think I did. He was too good for you." A concession, "In spite of your many faults, I would miss you. And with Vincent gone again."

"He comes back, will again. He'll get hungry and be at the door, and we'll take him in, as always."

"I'll never understand him."

"Nor I." The scramble for sainthood in older generations was marked by an obligation to God to assume responsibility for the eternal salvation of loved ones, an onerous duty with one's salvation at stake. Families suffered this interference, suffered the quarrels, the bickering, the license for criticism as attributes of 'this veil of tears'. From such a tradition Hannah's next parley came easily, "You spanked him too much."

"You spanked yours."

"For kid stuff, yes. We all did that. But I'd see you spank him for reasons that I, honest to God, could not figure out. The rest of them used to say that it was for that priest stuff."

"We're back to that."

Hannah watched her sister for a long time, waited for her to talk, to defend herself, even admit her worries, but Emma remained silent. Hannah ventured, "There is something I'd like to know. Where did you get the notion that he wanted to be a priest? You never told me, you never told anyone, you always acted like he'd been born that way, like he'd been born with a tag on him, a tag stamped by God and saying 'Priest.'"

"Oh, Hannah! Such nonsense. You old fool!" Not a tag from God, no tag. Whenever she thought about it, she always saw the light, the white light falling across her beautiful son asleep in her arms, a ray of sunlight streaming through the white mantle of the Virgin in the stained glass window and shining upon her child who was about to be christened Vincent, Vincent of St. Vincent's Church where they stood, and the choice easy because the saint of his birthday was unknown to her, or a foreign and unpretty name. And the old priest had smiled, blessing the child Vincent, "With such a name, maybe a priest? The priest we need, the priest from our own parish, the priest I'm sure you want. He'll be your blessing." She believed it. And Vincent's brightness and beauty, those gifts from God, were cherished, carefully encouraged, and made worthy of the apostolic life. He was set apart, the example for all in the parish school, the pious nuns knowing nothing of, or choosing to ignore the envy, the jealousy, the all of those Seven Sins nurtured by such idolatry. Emma knew of it, was told of it, told again today, knew of the resentment, even from family.

So sure of his budding priest, the pastor of St. Vincent's wangles a four-year scholarship out of parish funds and an obliging bishop. So Vincent became the charge of the Jesuits, who for their own reasons tolerated his poor scholarship and his arrogance for four years of preparatory school and permission to enroll at their university. One semester of his drinking and brawling, his skipping classes, ended Vincent's college career. Secretly pleased as they may have been, the family took him in, found jobs for him, welcomed him home, and understood his drinking.

If Emma ever told anyone why her Vincent was to have become a priest, she then would have had to explain why God had decided against him, and this she did not know.

> <u>Omaha World Herald:</u> *Services are pending for Vincent O'Meara of Council Bluffs. Mr. O'Meara died suddenly in Las Vegas, Nevada. A veteran of the Vietnam War, he is survived by his mother, Mrs. Emma O'Meara of Council Bluffs, an Aunt, and one son of Bassett, Nebraska.*

"This church funeral is not right! It's a sacrilege! He hasn't seen the inside of a church in years. Or was there big reconciliation you failed to tell me about?"

"No, nothing like that! It's what I want, what I think is right!" Emma refused to quarrel with Hannah, but she would silence her, "You and your big church talk, always back to that! When did they make you Pope?"

"Oh, Emma, I don't really care." Tearfully, she offered, "I don't want to make things harder for you, but he left the Church years ago, and now here you are bringing him back. Don't the dead's wishes mean anything any more?"

Now Emma was crying at her kitchen table, papers spread before her, vital statistics, the obituary, insurance forms. And just herself to do it. Hannah questioning every decision.

"I wish I could just have him decently boxed and put into the ground. It's what he would have wanted and all I really want." Emma had said this to the undertaker in that awful room of caskets, but he too had forms, legalities, regulations, the notice for the newspaper. Some Army officer had called. The church part had been the easiest, the baptism and first communion records still there, needing only a call to the chancery office.

Suddenly, in that odd mix of emotions that claim mourners, alternately weeping and laughing, Emma smiled, "Yes, he left the Church—many times, but he always came back. What I'm doing is the coming back for him one last time."

A call from Sister Theresa. Vincent was being kept after school for this latest infraction. "And there might be further disciplinary action, Mrs. O'Meara. This behavior will not be tolerated! We can expel him, you know."

The nun had sent the offensive magazine home with him, it carefully concealed in an old newspaper. His teacher had found it in his geography book. The spanking Emma gave him was severe. She had to make him cry, knew that if she did not, he would try this trick again.

A fierce quarrel that night, accusations thrown at a father, "Too easy on him! Letting him go in that back room at Ed's! Your brother and that trash he keeps back there! Not fit for a man, let alone a boy!"

Emma remembered that incident as the first time Vincent left the Church. He came to the kitchen the next morning, still in his pajamas, and announced defiantly that he would never go to that 'damned school again! That damned school and it's damned teachers! So there!'

By this time, Emma was feeling guilty about the spanking, so she took him in her arms and told him he could stay home as long as he wanted. After an idle two days, he was ready to return to school and church again.

Emma explained to Hannah, "He left the Church that time over a girlie magazine."

"Good God! How old was he?"

"I think seventh grade. He found it in that back room of Ed's drug store; you know the trash Ed used to keep back there. Vinnie took it to school to show it off, and one of the nuns found it."

"And you spanked him?"

"I thought I had to."

"Did it cure him?"

"You and your smart questions! Of course it did not cure him! Go look if you must. Look upstairs, they're still there, stashed away, been there for years."

"I've seen them. Pretty tame stuff to what we see today." Grief rode hard on Hannah. Sometimes, when she could stand it no longer, she would turn to silliness.

"While we're at it, let's take one of the newer ones, a really wild one, and bury it with him. Put it in his coat pocket! A tidbit for St. Peter."

"A tidbit for St. Peter! Now who's being sacrilegious?"

"The sight of a woman's body offensive in the eye of God?" Hannah debated, then, offered, "I expect there are those who'd argue with that."

The bells at the front door rang loudly, designed so that Emma could hear them from wherever she might be working. This was her favorite of the three houses that she owned, all of them Victorians with high ceilings, lustrous wood, leaded windows and wide staircases leading to the apartments upstairs. She and Hannah were comfortable on the first floor, their bedrooms a former library and a former back parlor. She found Nick Turner at the door. She had been expecting him.

"Elsie sent over these rolls…wants to know if you need anything…" Nick was shy, spluttered, "So few of us left…the old neighborhood so changed."

Emma reassured him, "So good of you to come, Nick. Come to the kitchen. Hannah and I are having some tea."

Turner sat with the two women, had tea and cookies, talked of old times and of Vinnie. His talk irritated Hannah, she was glad to see the last of him as he found his way down the back steps.

"What's wrong with that man? He was jittery as a cat! Him and his silly talk! Did he even know Vinnie?"

"He has good reason to be jittery around me," Emma explained, "Fact is, I'm surprised he showed up at all. Elsie must have made him come, and yes, he did know Vinnie."

"Why the fidgets?"

"He has a son Vinnie's age—the Ralph I asked him about. He works downtown, is doing well."

Hannah waited for more, but Emma's mind seemed to be elsewhere. Impatient, Hannah demanded, "Emma, for God's sake, what's the story?"

"Story? Well, I suppose you could call it that. The truth is, it's about another time that Vinnie left the Church, this time because he had been sent to jail."

"Jail! For what?"

"He wasn't there very long. I had Father Pat get him out."

"Where was your Len?"

"This was a year or two after Len died—seems to me Vinnie was in college, or I thought he was in college. He and Ralph Turner were pretty thick at the time."

"Ralph go to jail, too?"

"No, just Vinnie. They said he cheated at cards, somebody called the police, and then accused Vinnie of stealing money."

"Vinnie cheating at cards? I find that hard to believe. He didn't need to cheat, was good enough to win without it. My Will claimed he could have made a living playing cards."

"Well, maybe. I think Vin believed that himself, at least for a time he did, started playing poker in grade school, thanks to his Uncle Ed."

"Ed was a sly one."

"Yes, Vinnie came by it honestly. After this fracas, he got away from both me and the police. Went to New Orleans."

"Emma!" Hannah snapped, "You can be so aggravating when you set out to protect him, like now. Your mind goes all over the place. Tell me, did Vinnie really cheat, or steal? And what does Nick Turner have to do with all of this."

"Well, it took some time for me to figure it out, had to put it together myself. At first, I couldn't understand why Vin was so mad at me about Father Pat, but then, shortly after this jail thing, Ralph Turner got married, and a little too soon after that Nick and Elsie had their first grandchild. Elsie and I put it together, figured that the priest got the story out of Ralph. He's the one who needed the twenty-five dollars. There was that woman over on South Third who did that operation."

"The only thing I got out of Vinnie was being told to keep my damned priests out of his life, and that he could get himself out of jail without their help, or mine."

"You don't need to send shoes, you know." Hannah limping, getting in the way, but determined to help.

"I know that…you forget this is not the first time for me, even back to Pa—you were the oldest, but you were worthless, couldn't help with anything, crying all over the place, crying then, crying now. You must stop it, you're wearing me out with it, and you're making yourself sick…Hannah…Hannah!"

"Don't be cross with me. I can't stop crying, and you know too, it should be me, not Vinnie—it's more my turn. What is God thinking of?"

"Quit that. It's bad enough with that talk, and you want to help, help me with this tie. Will it do, will it go all right with that shirt?"

"Yes, yes, I think so, but I still think it should be his uniform. They can cut the back—no one would see."

"No, Hannah. Not that."

"T'would be more fitting and easier."

"Don't argue. It will be the suit." Choked with tears, Emma's voice faded, was almost a whisper, "There won't be that many to see, with just you and me left."

"Nobody from out of town?"

"They're just cousins, scattered all over, and we've been out of touch for years." Emma was brushing the lint from a coat. Her voice faded to a whisper, "Unless the boy comes…and his mother…but I doubt that."

Hannah stared at her. She knew Emma could be secretive, exasperatingly so with Vinnie's escapades. Now Emma's words told her that something very grave had been kept from her. Vincent had a son, a son he had never seen, a son hidden from her. The words were like a slap in the face for Hannah. Emma had not trusted her, had shut her out like a stranger. She waited, torn with anger and disappointment, she managed only, "Boy?"

"Yes, must be almost a man by now."

"That old?" Hannah probed carefully, but with some bite, "Where have you got him stashed away?"

Emma ignored the sting, said only, "I have never seen him myself."

"My God!" Hannah gasped, "I've always known you were a hard woman, Emma, but this is the worst! Not seen your only grandchild! Why? Where is he?"

"He lives on a ranch in Nebraska. They raise cattle."

Hannah exploded, "You stand there, your only child dead, and you talk about a grandson you have never seen! Like he is nothing to you! That's not normal, Emma! You're not normal! What in God's name is wrong with you?"

Emma retaliated, "Hannah! This is bad enough without your constantly turning on me! So quick to judge, and so quick to blame! Can't you just once be with me? Just once know that I did the right thing!"

Tears were streaming from Emma's eyes, "Do you really believe that I would willingly give up a grandchild? How could you? My God, you must hate me!"

Shocked, stunned by blame and guilt, Hannah could only stare at Emma who was insisting, "Well, hate me or not, blame me, blame me if you will, but you understand right now that I did not abandon that little boy, that between Vinnie and the child's grandfather all I got to do was pay the god-damned bills!"

Hannah retreated, silenced by the force of Emma's anger. An anger new to Hannah. Emma had always been calm, controlled, the widowed sister who, much to the family's relief, had survived on her own. Emma, ordinary Emma, whose successes Hannah had labeled stubbornness, whose prosperity Hannah had tolerated as stinginess, and whose caring for a disabled old woman and a dissolute son had been accepted as 'doing her Christian duty'. Suddenly, Hannah was frightened. She had lost something.

This day ended the world of Vincent O'Meara. He had been born at an unlucky time, a turning point for a culture, a time when survival for that culture demanded reform. Any change was anathema to a man whose spiritual birthright, whose soul was embedded in the old order with its holy wars, those fought in bars, in the streets, in the bedroom, and with an awful accountability that Vincent O'Meara simultaneously loved and feared. He never resolved his own inner struggle between that which strengthened and that which enfeebled.

Emma O'Meara had seen all of this, and had understood its truth, had understood her son's failures, and long before this day, she had schooled herself to salvage him again and again without expecting any return in kind. She had long known that his failures kept her the specter in her son's life, just as she understood that Hannah's poverty drained her of any charity she might have had for the woman who cared for her. But on this day of death, Emma defended herself against Hannah's charge of wickedness. Slowly, deliberately, she related the story of her grandson's birth, explaining that the girl's father did not believe in divorce. The girl had run away from home to find work in Omaha. She was only seventeen when she met Vincent O'Meara, just home from Vietnam, his severance pay and his poker winnings in his pocket. The money lasted two months. Her father found the new Mrs. O'Meara pregnant and abandoned in an apartment in West Omaha.

"A divorce would have been easier, but her father insisted on an annulment, threatened charges against Vinnie without it. The annulment was expensive and it took two years, but it meant a good home for my grandson, that and my and Vinnie's promise to stay out of his life. He has been well cared for.

"And Vinnie? Vinnie went back to the Church again, this time to a monastery someplace in Missouri. You can read the card he sent me. I still have it."

Liddy and Company

"That's it. Ain't no more I can do."

Out of breath from wrestling with a snow rug by the front door, Liddy had stopped for a quick peak into an antique mirror that hung near the stairway. Her hand jabbed once, then again at a strand of hair. She captured the wayward lock in the loop of a wire hairpin, flattened it against her head only to have it escape and swing free once more.

"Damn!"

She glared at the mirror and once more aimed the hairpin, but her hand wavered and dropped to her side. She moaned, "Who'll notice?"

A cake reflected in the mirror had brought back the morning's failure. 'Trying to be the fancy cook, which I ain't—Mrs. Highfallutin. The blasted thing falling in the pan and tasting awful. Of course he had to come along and catch me throwing it out.'

"By God, we can't afford to throw out good food! Do you think I'm made of money?"

A quick step to Sophie's chickens had rid her of the offensive cake, but the uneasiness and the guilt remained.

'It's the mess, the mess of the guilt frames fillin' up the dinin' room somethin' he has no part of, but must put up with. No use telling him he doesn't make a quilt cause ye needs it so much as ye needs the makin' of it. Spose now I'll hafta give the blasted thing t'Nell after telling him I would. She allus were his favrit.'

"Ma, why don't you throw that damned old mirror out? You glare and rag at it like it's something you hate!"

Startled by Helen's sudden appearance, and her blasphemy, Liddy reprimanded her daughter, "Throw it out! And after yer grandmother bringin' it all the ways from the old country? Here all this time I thought ye'd be proud t'own it someday!"

"It's old, it's ugly, it makes you look ugly, get rid of it!"

"No. It ain't the mirror I'm frowning at, it's that hank of hair. I can't get to lay down, see if y'can fix it…oh, never mind, there's the front door and Soph's comin' up the back path."

The arrival of her friends banished Liddy's gloom, that and the satisfaction of knowing that her house was ready for those critical glances from old eyes long the enemies of dust and cobwebs. And she especially enjoyed a quilting, looked forward to the bits and pieces of gossip, the intimacies of women with their shy explorations of 'female' troubles, both sins and illnesses, subjects not openly discussed in Liddy's day. Such subjects were private, taboo, possibly immoral, but in the coziness of a quilting, one dared much.

Even the stings of Jo, Liddy's sister-in-law, seemed to be blunted in the closeness of a quilting.

Ellie Pearson started the conversation, once the women were settled around the quilt frame. Pretty as a girl, Ellie had not acquired the inhibitions that less attractive women collect as they seek acceptance in society. Accordingly, unfettered by self-criticism, Ellie adroitly avoided all intellectual challenges, even card-playing which she labeled the 'Devil's work'. A handsome matron, she philosophically faced like assured that any adversity was 'the Lord's will'. She described her own plumpness with a good-natured, "If the Lord'd intended me t'be skinny, he'd a made me skinny." Thus allied with divine providence, she spoke her mind freely and often. Now her short, agile fingers worked in the February sun pushing the needle in and out, up and down the penciled arches.

"Ye made a good match with me brown paisley, Liddy."

Pleased, Liddy squinted across the quilt in Ellie's direction, "Yes, I scrounged a long time fer that orange, don't much care fer the color m'self, but it worked in good there."

"Well, everra time y'snuggles down at night, y'can think a me 'n have a good laugh. Buyin' that place at Thorson's jest cause t'were on sale, 'n then havin t'live with it years on end."

"Not me snugglin'. Nell gets this." Aware of special news about Liddy's oldest daughter, the women waited only to have Liddy change the subject.

"So curious 'bout that quilt that Margaret's making. I hear 'tis something grand. A'course I never was one t'visit much with 'em, but I thought mebbe you'd seen it, Ellie. Or you, Soph. You been over there lately, will she be wantin' us t'quilt it?"

"That'll be the day."

"Now, Helen," Sophie chided her young neighbor. She continued, "I was there last week and 'tis near done. She ain't said nothing 'bout quiltin it, but my, tis a grand sight, all them colors and that shiny satin, kinda reminds a body of the windas in the church."

"Humph!" Jo sniffed. Jo had never married. A thin, bony woman, she sat erect, her graying hair tightly braided and shaped into a beehive mound. She wore small gold-rimmed glasses pinched to her nose and held safe by a black retractable ribbon pinned to her shirtwaist. Her dark eyes swept the circle of faces before her, then lowered as she sniffed again, "She spends 'nuff time there, she'd oughta be able t'match 'em. But," now with raised eyebrows, "who ever heard a makin' a satin quilt, how'll she clean it?"

Sophie defended against Margaret Thorson, "Jo, y'knows verra well she only took on that church work afta Jed's Ma died." Looking directly at the culprit, Sophie continued, "Margaret is different from us, we all knows that, but she thought a lot of Jed's Ma, is makin' the quilt outta her dresses it's like she's keeping something t'remember her with."

The kindly grandmother leaned back from her sewing, her eyes still on Jo while she said to the others, "I don't know as y'all know 'bout 'em, but Jed's Pa'd bring her one of them fancy things everra time he'd make a buy'in trip. Sometimes when I was there with the eggs she'd show 'em t'me, kinda struttin' like she allus did. I liked looking at 'em 'n if she was a proud woman I guess she had reason 'nuff t'be. And now them things is in a quilt."

Sophie chuckled, "Heaven knows I ain't proud, can't afford t'be, 'n I learned long ago t'be satisfied with what I got. 'Magine me, all decked out in satin in the hen coop!"

"Well, God knows she stayed well away from hen coop 'n a lotta other places the rest of us have had t'put up with."

"Ye'll hafta 'mit though, Ellie, God rest her soul, she was a good woman in her own way, and I think Margaret's a lot like her."

Ellie agreed, "I spose yer right, Soph, and if Margaret wants a fancy quilt she's got the house fer it." Then, slyly, "Didja rekanize Ma's purple petticoat in it?"

Liddy gasped, "Ellie, ye didn't! Ye didn't give away that petticoat! The purple one y'kept fer so long? Yer own Ma's?" Liddy smiled, remembering, "I kin see her yet, so light on her feet, 'n the sound a that taffety n' the peak of that ruffle, showin' out from under her skirt!" Liddy paused, embarrassed, but she admitted, "Ain't it funny? I was jest little, but I'd; 'magine m'self dancin', dancin' like a princess, dancin' in a purple ruffly petticoat."

Ellie teased, "T'would take more'n a fancy petticoat t'lighten yer feet, Liddy!" A sigh, then, "But 'twas getting frayed 'n I was tired a packin' it away, 'n y'know, really, I'm kinda proud t'have something a Ma's in something so fine."

"Sadie McGuire's yellow silk is in there, too."

Helen kept her eyes on the quilt. Liddy glared at her. Shocked silence. Sophie quickly changed the subject, "I d'clare that blasted thread's broke again. Would y'mind threadin it fer me, Ellie? M'eyesight's getting so poo 'n loolin' in this sun's made it worse."

Ellie reached for Sophie's needle, "If y'd push yer glasses back t'where they belongs, ye wouldn't have no trouble." She looked meaningfully at Helen while she spoke, "Nobody that makes stitches so fine 'n even as you is havin' trouble with her eyes, Soph."

"Mebbe, but I'm getting older, y'knows, time t'quit some of these fancy things." Sophie persisted, keeping the conversation away from talk of Sadie McGuire. For Sophie the 'doins of such as that woman ain't fit talk for decent company." She inquired of Liddy, "So this quilt's fer Nell. Does I hear rightly? Is she that way agin?"

Liddy moaned, "Yes, 'n that big old house's so cold. I told her not to let Hugh buy it, knowing him and that family he comes from he'll jest break his neck t'fill it."

"T'ain't his neck that's getting..."

"Jo!"

"My, ain't we the uppity one! I spose the stork brot those six a yourn, Ellie."

"Fer a woman that ain't never married y'got a wise tongue on ye, Jo." Then Ellie announced, "I'll tell ye one thing I learned and learned long ago, and that is I don't talk 'bout him and he don't talk 'bout me!" She added smugly, "Better'n some peoples I knows."

Jo, always impatient with innuendo, ordered, "Speak yer piece, Ellie."

"Well," Ellie paused, straightened her shoulders, glanced around the table, savoring the drama, "Satedy night Jamie stopped in at the pool hall fer some beer, and you-know-who was there, drinkin' and talking terrible." Her plump fist hit the quilt emphatically, I'll tell yez one thing...if my man ever...ever!...called me a cold fish, I'd leave him!"

"Ye shouldn't be repeatin' things like that, Ellie."

"Oh, Soph, it's all over town".

In Sophie's busy life there was little time for philosophical musings or speculations. She had always been poor and hard working, but she accepted her way of life as God's plan for her and believed that envy of the prosperous offended Him. But she did expect Christian behavior from the well to do, the Thorson family in particular. Now she shook her head, upset by behavior from a man who should 'know better' than to talk about his home life with cheap boozers. She shook her head, rationalized, "Trouble with Jed is he's too hansum fer his own good and he's allus had it so easy, his Pa settin' him up in that store n'all. But he was sech a good little boy, so polite when I'd be there visitin' with his Ma." She stopped, studied her hands as they smoothed the wrinkles from the quilt, then continued, "It's allus kinda bothered me, though, Jed getting married so young, don't think he was quite ready for it."

Liddy offered, "He was almost nineteen when he got married, Soph. His and Helen's birthday's the same week."

"That's right. I'd forgot." Jo squinted at Helen, "'N wasn't ye kinda sweet on him, Helen?" Helen glared at Jo who went on blithely, "Now don't blush, tain't no sin to fall in love, 'n someday yer man'll come along."

"I'm not holding my breath waiting for him Aunt Jo!" Helen was furious, "And I'm not blushing! I never cared that much for Jed Thorson!" Defiantly, she added, "At least not enough to lower myself to catch him the way some people I know would!"

In a sing-song voice like that of a child with a school yard victory, Jo reprimanded her niece, "If ye was as good at countin' stitches as ye is at countin' months we wouldn't be waitin fer ye everra time we's ready to start a new row." Then, pointedly, "Y'knows that child was premature."

"I know nothing of the sort, and I don't care," Helen mocked her aunt, "You're the one who has to know everything about everybody and that ought to make you blush, Jo."

Jo heard Liddy's gasp and retreated, "Aw, Helen, my blushin' days are far behind me, and besides what's wrong with some interest in other folks' affairs?' Her voice softened, "I don't really care whether Margaret's baby came too soon or not, but would ye be wantin' me t'be like Mrs. Mac there? Allus so quiet, hardly hears nothing."

Liddy, "Be careful, Jo, it may be one of her good days."

Ruth McIntosh, partially deafened by a childhood disease, smiled at Jo. She had heard the 'Mac' and tried to join the conversation, "Eh, what's that you say, Jo? What about spring?"

Jo, adeptly, "I think t'will be early this year, time t'start sortin' seeds fer plantin'."

The deaf woman leaned forward, "Pantin'? Who's pantin'?"

Ellie took over, "Me. I'm pantin'. Liddy, the sun shinin' on these pieces is bringin' out the smell of mothballs. Ye musta had some of 'em put away fer years." She fanned herself, "We've finished this line and I know it's early, but don't yez thinks it's time fer coffee? I needs t'smell something diff'runt."

"Yer right, Ellie. Helen, Soph'll finish yer line whiles ye help me in the kitchen."

Helen, still stinging from Jo's talk, quickly rose and followed her mother. Liddy shook the grate of the old wood range as she inwardly searched for 'the right words'. She hated scenes, could not tolerate anger, anyone's anger, but before she could speak Helen hissed in her ear, "Ma, why do you do this to me? Dragging me out here like a ten-year-old! Don't you trust me with dear Aunt Jo?"

"Hush, they'll hear yez. I needs more cobs t'make this water boil. Put some in the end there."

"There! There's your cobs! Now what? Why don't you call that old maid out here and shut her up? Dear Aunt Jo! No wonder she never married, that tongue of hers would scare any man!"

The words were old. Liddy had heard them before, had said them herself, but she warned her daughter, "Hush, she's got ears like a cat and she is your Pa's sister."

Helen banged the stove lid down, "Well, tell her to leave me alone or I will!" In a strained whisper she charged at Liddy, at her aunt, at her father, "I'm tired of hearing that old story of Grandpa chasing every man off the place. No one good enough for her! Was there anybody to chase? Is that what they'll say about me?"

"Helen, again I'm tellin' yez t'shush!" Pushed too far, Liddy snapped at her daughter, "Yer getting jest like her!"

"After a cup of coffee 'n some of yer pound cake we'd ought t'be able t'finish that row this afternoon." Sophie was finding her place at the kitchen table, "Or is it yer pound cake, Lid?"

"Yes, it's the pound cake agin," Liddy admitted, "I tried that white cake res'pee a Millie McPeek's, but it fell and tasted so funny I had t'throw it out."

Ellie laughed, "Millie? You'd oughta known by now not t'trust her. She never gives a res'pee straight!"

Laughing at this joke, the women found their places at the round oak table. Sophie, who liked Helen very much, drew her into the conversation. "It must be yer afternoon off, Helen. How's the job comin'?"

"Oh, fine, Soph. It was confusing for a while but now I know the switchboard, so it's easy and really kind of fun." Proud of her work, Helen explained, "Do you know we've got over a hundred phones in town and getting more from the farms all of the time?"

"Fancy that. A hunert?" Sophie did not have a telephone, nor did she want one. She labeled the telephone as 'some kind of gadget movin in on yez, like having a stranger in the house'. But she was very comfortable with moral issues, particularly with what she called 'wimmins' place. Now she probed, cautiously, careful not to upset Liddy, "How many days does ye work? Wensdy's kind of a funny day t'have off, does that means ye works Sundays?"

"Yes, and I was alone last Sunday for the first time."

Sophie and her friends 'kept the Sabbath', but all of them listened politely as Helen continued, "Sadie says I'm good enough now so she can take some time off, and she's promised me the night shift. It's less work than days, but it pays a little better."

Sophie persisted. She had strong opinions about women working outside of the home, days or nights, but now she spoke only about dangers, "I'd hate t'be down there alone at night. Won't yez be scared?"

"Soph, I like the work, and I'll get used to being alone. It's all lit up and right down town. The night watchman keeps an eye on the building." Helen regretted adding, "There's a cot so I can sleep when the lines are quiet."

Jo smirked, "We all know how that cot keeps Sadie McGuire from being scared." Ignoring the shocked silence of the others, Jo rattles on, "I don't know as I'd be wantin' a daughter of mine t' be socializin with the likes of a woman like her." Understanding Liddy and her friends very well, Jo dared more, "Ye never did tell us how that yellow silk got in Margaret Thorson's quilt."

"I figured you'd have to know that, Jo." Then, defiantly, "It got there because I gave it to her. Sadie gave it to me, but the color was wrong, so when I was helping Margaret cut some pieces I asked her if she wanted it." Helen ended with a barbed, "Sadie's got as nice clothes as anyone you'll ever know."

Jo salvaged what she could, "Well, I'm glad ye's a good friend with Margaret. This family could use some refinement. She is a real lady."

Jo had one more pronouncement, "And Jed Thorson needs his mouth washed out with soap."

The quilters finished their afternoon quietly, steadily sewing, talking only about families or housework, safe topics, the gossip of early afternoon tucked away for home and evening, and husbands. By four o'clock, the snow outside no longer filled the room with reflected light, and the penciled lines were becoming hard to see in the shadowy patches of the quilt. Jo offered Mrs. Mac a ride home in her Model T, and Helen walked Ellie home, wanting some time outside on her afternoon off. Sophie stayed to help Liddy with the kitchen cleanup.

The two women had been neighbors for twenty years, backdoor neighbors, a relationship distinctly their own, a rich and subtle kinship, female. Liddy's kitchen was as familiar to Sophie as her own, and in an easy silence the two friends cleaned, washed away all traces of the party, readied the room for supper. Sophie sighed as she wrapped her shawl around her shoulders.

"Tired, Soph?"

"No, that ain't it." Shaking her head, Sophie confided, "Life does funny things t'ye Lid. I used t'think t'would be great when the kids was growed and outta the way and I c'd spend m'time visitin' and bein' with m'friends." She brushed back a strand of white hair that had fallen across her glasses, "But it don't feel the way I thought t'would."

"What's on yer mind?"

"Well fer one thing and you c'n tell me it ain't none o' me business and I spose it ain't, but does it bother ye that Helen ain't married yet?"

"Yes, it bothers me some." Certain troubles, problems in family life were held to be sacred, not fit for talk with any one other than family. Economic failures, some illnesses, alcoholism, were not admitted openly as families feared pain or censure of loved ones if secrets were exposed. Now, Sophie's question was trespass, 'goin' too far', but she touched a real worry. The changes in Helen, her continued single state, the undercurrent of criticism from Jo, all nagged at Liddy, isolated her from Helen and from Helen's father. She felt alone, uncertain about her own life, could see no change, just an ongoing dreariness in the future. She needed to talk, needed Sophie's steadiness.

"Soph, I like having Helen home, and she is so excited about this job. Mebbe the real trouble is that you'n me was brought up hearin' the words 'old maid' so often, like 'twas the worst thing that c'd happen. And really, the truth is she's better off than Nell, working dawn t'dusk, and with another one comin'." Liddy paused, and then allowed herself the luxury of anger, "I'll tell yez one thin' though, Soph, I c'd jest wring Jo's neck. Sometimes I wants t'tell her ta jest shut up and leave Helen alone, then I tells m'self that that'd be putting too much 'mportance t'it."

"Well, that's the kinda stuff I mean, makes me feel edgy and nervous. That and that talk 'bout Margaret and Jed Thorson."

"Are ye worried 'bout 'em, Soph? They ain't havin' real troubles is they? Really?"

Sophie frowned, "I don't think so. I don't go over there as much as I used t'afore Jed's Ma died, but when I go everrathins so bright and pretty, 'n she seems so happy t'have some one t'come and see her." Soph brightened, "She's a hard worker, Liddy, keeps that house jest shinin', 'n I don't think she has much hired help."

Jed's mother had been one of the few women in the community to have regular household help, her money setting her apart from many women. Liddy asked quickly, "Ain't Jed doin' well at the store?"

"Oh, I don't think 'tis nothing like that. A course Jed likes t'spend it, but so'd his Pa." Sophie continued, "What's really botherin' me is that story Ellie told. Does yer Pete ever say anythin' 'bout Jed drinkin too much. Had ye heard that story afore?"

"Oh, Soph, I wouldn't pay no mind t'talk like that."

Sophie was not to be dismissed, "Ye had heard it then."

"I didn't say that. All I'm sayin' who knows what a man'll say when he's had too much." Liddy tried to be reassuring, "It's probly jest a story those old stewbums made up. That's why I'm glad my Pete don't go there much. The way I hears it, they talks terrible 'bout everaabody, worse than the barbershop. Helen says that's where that 'bout Sadie McGuire got started."

"Sadie shouldn't dress so fancy. I didn't think that job paid that well." Sophie tried to be fair, "But she is a hansum woman. Spose if I were that hansum I'd put everra penny on m'back, too, but let's hope that same talk don't get goin' about Helen. She's a mighty pretty girl, too, Lid."

"Yes, and she's a good girl, and if she wants t'be an old maid that's all right with me. At least she's seen 'nuff a her Aunt Jo not t'be like her, all dried up inside, settin' out there on that farm trying t'run everrabody's bizness jest cause she'd got a little money."

Sophie hung a wet towel to dry, looked toward the window, saying, "I see Helen's comin' back, and I'd best be getting home." Pullin' her shawl close to her shoulders, she ended the afternoon's talk, "Guess I'm jest tired t'day, letting that talk bother me. Febawary's a funny month fer me, seems like I'm allus strainin' t'keep busy—one thing, Margaret's quilt. Don't be sprised she don't want us t'help. She's diffrunt, awful persnickety 'bout what's hers."

Jo was wrong. Spring was late. February's snows clung to the ground until April, darkened and smudged by a March of little change, just a succession of drab days with no clean new snow, nor no warmth to make the gray snow disappear. Liddy fretted, disappointed about Margaret's quilt, 'Thinks she's too good fer us, I guess.' She complained about the cold and the dampness that kept doors closed, 'meant t'varnish that parlor woodwork this spring and Helen's room needs calcimining, now spring cleanin's goin' t'run into gardenin', how's a body to cope?' The confinement, the cold, the dark skies defeated any gestures toward change. In late March, Nell lost her baby. Standing in the sleet at the cemetery service, Liddy wondered why she herself cried so little, why the helplessness and beauty of the tiny body had stirred only a moment's tear, why she felt only relief that her daughter had been spared the burden of another child too soon. Liddy's depression deepened as she watched Helen comfort Nell. Would Helen never have a child of her own?

Jo dispatched Liddy's melancholy with her proposal at the family dinner after the funeral.

"He may seem a little slow, but I think that's mostly cause he's shy. He's steady and he's a hard worker, don't drink nor smoke and y'can be sure ye'll never have t'worry 'bout him chasin' other wimmin." Jo ended with a flourish, "'N that way mebbe I c'an see m'way clear t'givin' ye the farm."

Liddy had not shared her concerns about Helen with her husband, believing that he would dismiss her worries as troublemaking. Now, she let him stumble up Jo's path alone.

"He'd be awfully good to you, Helen."

"Sven? Pa!" Helen faced her father, "Are you that desperate to get me married?"

Her thoughts on Jo's oafish hired man, Liddy missed the shocked look on her husband's face, but she heard the slam of Helen's door upstairs. With a glance at the culprit, Liddy guessed that Jo had discussed the proposed match with Helen's father.

Helen was working nights while Sadie McGuire was on a vacation trip to St. Louis. 'I spose t'put more clothes on her back,' Liddy mused to herself. She was talking to herself much of the time as few of her friends had telephones. Helen was distant with her, too. 'Probly thinks I put Jo up t'it, and that I side with her Pa.' She learned that Helen often stopped for a quick visit with Margaret

Thorson after a night at the switchboard. Secretly, Liddy worried about the town's gossips, 'that damned bed down there', so she was relieved that it was the respectable Margaret to whom Helen had turned.

Relentless Jo, however, interpreted Helen's actions in her own way. She had come early one morning and visited with Liddy until Helen walked in the door.

"I hears yer comin' to yer senses, Helen. Yer Ma tells me yer seein' a lot a Margaret Thorson, so you's must be getting over bein' jealous a her cause she got Jed." Jo swept on in spite of Helen's gasp, "Now yer friends with her and 'tis time, too, fer ye t'see ye c'n do jest as well. Sven is a good worker, 'n with that farm, in time c'd be real well off." She added smugly, "'N someday have jest as nice as Margaret's!"

Helen exploded, "Aunt Jo, I am not now, nor never have been jealous of Margaret Thorson!" She defied Jo, "And you can keep your damned old farm! Pa'll get it some day anyway!" She was merciless, "You're stuck with it! You're living on it and you're stuck out there alone with Sven! Marry him yourself!"

Halfway up the stairs to her room, Helen turned and faced the two women, "And I think it's time some of you old busybodies learned the truth about your Margaret Thorson!"

Liddy looked at Jo, braced herself for accusations from a woman she neither liked nor trusted. She was unprepared for Jo's, "I done me best."

Liddy stood at the window for a long time, watched long after the Model T disappeared from view, then turned fitfully to her day's work, in a now lonely house. Throughout the morning she returned again and again to the window as if looking for something, something lost, taken from her, gone with the Ford. The Jo in the Model T, the Jo who loved Helen as a stranger, far different from the long-cherished specter that Liddy had brought with her to her marriage bed. She called it 'puttin' up with Jo', a Christian woman's duty to an old maid sister-in-law. Liddy sought that specter all morning, rehashed old arguments, relived old hurts, justified old hates, only to have to admit that the witch, Jo, the evil-doer, the manipulator was gone, had never been. All that remained of that Jo was Liddy's humiliation. She tried to escape her thoughts, found herself twice at the door only to remember that Sophie was gone for the day, sewing for grandchildren. Several times she started up the stairs for 'a good talk' with Helen, but each time turned back, unsure of herself, unready for what was surely a 'diffrunt' Helen.

Morning brought a bright sun, warmth, and Sophie hurrying around the ice-crusted puddles to reach Liddy's back door.

"Come in, Soph, come in," Liddy welcomed her, "I been looking for ye, set right there." Then seeing the distress in Sophie's face, she cried, "What's wrong, Soph? Yez looks awful!"

Sophie dropped to a chair, breathing heavily. Her words exploded before Liddy, "I'm in, I'm down, and I gotta talk t'Helen! Is she here? Call her, get her down here!"

"Helen's here, but she's asleep." Liddy asked, "c'n ye tell me what you want? Y'seems so worked up, is something wrong?"

"What's wrong is she's got to go t'her! Gotta t'go right now! Get her up Lid!"

Liddy, thoroughly confused, "Her? Who's her?"

Sophie was not listening. She rocked back and forth in the chair then stopped suddenly to point a finger at Liddy, "Ye'll never believe it! Never have I been talked to n'sech a way! She's gone mad! Yes, that's it, she's gone crazy!"

"Crazy? Who? Who's crazy? Soph, listen! Make sense!"

"Margaret! Margaret Thorson!"

"Oh, now, Soph, Helen was there this morning! That can't be! Calm down, yer ravin'."

"I ain't ravin'!" Sophie was shouting, "I ain't ravin'! I'm tellin' ye we's gotta do somethin' right away afore she hurts herself! Get Helen over there!"

An alarmed Liddy, "I ain't makin' a move till y'tells me what's happened! Now, slow down, start at the beginning!"

Sophie dropped her shoulders with a long sigh, "Liddy, y'knows I ain't the one t'interfere with the ways people lives, nor does I try t'tell em what t'do, but ye shoulda heard the thing she said t'me—ol' busybody, 'n livin' in the past, a pest! What kinda talk is that fer me who never wished her nothing but the best, n'all I was tryin' to do was t'make her stop!"

"Stop? Stop what?"

"The quilt! The quilt almost in shreds!" Sophie's voice was a near scream, "Great long cuts in it, tearin' n' laughin', 'n where's Helen? Get her over there! I think she's gone mad! 'N she shouldna talked t'me like that! I been friends of that fam'y fer years." Tears came to Sophie's eyes, "I mebbe ain't as good as they, but I never did 'spect' them t'bend t'me. I looked up t'them and helped 'em when I could 'n now t'be thrown otta the house by a woman gone mad, settin' there laughn' n' cuttin' 'n when I said somethin' turned on me like, like I was…" She stopped bewildered, "No matter what I was or is, I never chased nobody outta me own house with a sizzers in m'hand, no matter what she thinks a me!"

"A sizzers? Margaret?"

"Yes, and rippin' with her hands when the sizzer's didn't work! She's gone wild, Lid,' 'cause when I tried t'stop her she turned on me!"

"That don't make sense, Soph."

"I knows! I knows! First, I thought she was cryin'. I run right t'her, and then I seed she was laughin'. Then I knowed she'd gone mad. God knows what she'll do next!" Sophie was calmer, her words now a soft plea, "I think Helen c'n talk t'her, so get her up and send her over there."

"I ain't sendin' Helen to no crazy woman with a sizzers in her hand!" Alarmed, Liddy tried to think what to do, "I know, Jed! We'll get Jed! I'll call him at the store…let me see, whats the number…"

"T'ain't no use, Liddy! I'm tellin' ye, get Helen. Jed's gone, gone on a buyin' trip, I think t'St. Louis again. Helen knows that, now call her! Jed ain't home."

Liddy started for the stairs leading to Helen's room. She caught her image in the old mirror, saw the yellowed glass, the tarnished frame, and heard the words, 'time you old busybodies'. She turned back to Sophie, "Go home, Soph, go home and fergit the whole thing."

Sophie stared at her.

"Y'say's Jed's in St. Louie, 'n I knows Sadie McGuire's there, too. 'N something tells me that Margaret knows it…now, anyways…Helen musta told her." Liddy put the story together, "Yes, Margaret must know it, 'n my guess is that the sizzers 'n the quilt 'n the laughin' means she knows what t'do 'bout it." Liddy pressed Sophie's hand, "You 'n me 'n what we thinks 'bout the quilt, 'n Jed, 'n Jed's Ma, they ain't Margaret's ways, Soph. They're ourn. And they ain't workin' for her."

There was much speculation about what happened at the Thorson house that morning, few people knowing for sure. Phrases like 'a sizzers in her hand', 'blood all over the place', and 'went after the old lady' made the rounds, some talk about alcoholism, some about an 'uppity' family.

But the Thorson marriage flourished as did the store. Jed expanded a year later, most people thought it was his wife's doing, 'being the one who goes on those buying trips with him, finds all that new stuff he's doing so well with'.

Helen and Jo found many things they liked in Jed's new furniture department. Jo was doing over the farmhouse, remodeling and refurnishing it as a wedding gift for Helen and Sven.

Sophie's version of the altercation soon died out. Of course no one had ever asked Margaret what really happened, not even Helen. Her friendship with Margaret cooled some. After a few months Sophie got over her feelings about the Thorson's and went back to trading at their store. She's now finishing a satin baby quilt for Margaret and Jed's second child. Liddy's seen it, says "Tis something grand."

AN ARCHETYPAL CRITIQUE
THE SOUND AND THE FURY

At one time I approached the novels of William Faulkner to explore his statements on sex, hoping specifically to learn why we sense an ambivalence in his attitude toward virginity and to discover what statement he makes about promiscuity. In the three novels that I read, I could not come to a conclusive statement on sex in Faulkner's writing, but Caddy Compson of *The Sound and the Fury* emerged in my mind as a significant twentieth-century heroine. As a touchstone of tragedy, Caddy is more a presence than a character in the novel, a haunting sensual force suggestive of the classical beauty, Helen of Troy. In pursuing this parallel I discovered that an archetypal approach to the novel reveals that Faulkner had a rare understanding of a universal female posture and that his insight into the character of Helen may be the essence of amoral validity we find in his writings: this paper then will be a critique of *The Sound and the Fury* from an archetypal analysis.

As a character in classical literature, Helen of Troy actually has a small role, but she is the nucleus of a whole literary tradition. If a public moralist should say of her, "That bitch would live with any man," we should have to agree, but we would add that Meneleas was happy to have her return to him, and literature continues to welcome her back. Shakespeare calls her Gertrude; DeFoe, Moll Flanders. Blake analyzes her; tells us that if we treat her right, she is Ahania—wrong, and she is that witch Enitharmon. Faulkner loves her.

Caddy Compson as a character appears only briefly in *The Sound and the Fury*, but she too is the nucleus of tragedy, a provocative, almost primitive force that results in tragedy for those around her. With the stream-of-consciousness and personal narrative styles Faulkner reveals the inner conflict Caddy causes in the lives of her three brothers. The novelist is particularly skillful in this area as he gives a significant universality to the concept of Caddy by taking three men of completely diverse attitudes and capabilities and convincingly presents them as brothers. A culture as fragmented as the post-Civil War South allows him a strong element of credibility, and he ingeniously surrounds these men with directionless, ineffective characters—survivors merely waiting their lives out. The father has allowed his law practice to dwindle; the mother plays out her role as a Southern lady; an uncle is an inebriate; and an old negress manages all.

Benjy, an idiot in his thirties, is really a prototype of primate man, a man of limited intellectual ability whose responses are chiefly from his physical sensibilities. Mute, his disjointed impressions of life center around Caddy who 'smells like trees'. These words come when he seems to be in his most lucid, joyous moments, and he is upset when she wears perfume—a sophistication beyond his capabilities. His most vivid and repetitious memories are of the times that he was hurt or lost, and Caddy put her arms around him. Frogs, snakes, flowers, and the 'black ditch' are all associated in his mind with Caddy, indicating her primitive appeal. One of Benjy's few intellectual accomplishments is recognizing her name:

> "You just say it and see if he dont." Dilsey said. "You say it to him while he sleeping and I bet he hear you."[1]

Faulkner adds a temporal limitation to Caddy, which even primate man must experience:

> You cant do no good looking through the gate, T.P. said. Miss Caddy done gone long ways away. Done got married and left you. You cant do no good, holding to the gate and crying. She cant hear you.[2]

Benjy's Caddy is significantly physical, naturally sensual, maternally comforting: and separation from her is Benjy's recurring tragedy.

Quentin, the suicide, is the prototype of the intellectual, sensitive man. His Caddy is the Helen won by Meneleas, the ultimate feminine beauty coveted by all men. Faulkner adroitly uses the device of incest to keep his novel plausible and yet present the agony of desire that a beautiful woman can create in man.

---

1. William Faulkner, *The Sound and the Fury*, (Vintage Books, 1946), p. 37.
2. Ibid., p. 62

The incest is only in Quentin's mind, not in fact, emphasizing a pristine quality that beauty must have for a sensitive man. Quentin is the extreme opposite of Benjy, personifying the ritualistic ascetic who rejects life and is obsessed with death.

> But who loved death above all, who loved only death, loved and lived in a deliberate and almost perverted anticipation of death as a lover loves.[3]

Faulkner says that Quentin has a 'presbyterian' fear of eternal punishment, and the novelist insinuates the need for sacrificial offerings in Quentin's character.

> If it could just be a hell beyond that: the clean flame the two of us more than dead. Then you will have only me then only me then the two of us amid the pointing and the horror beyond the clean flame.[4]

Agonizing over Caddy's promiscuity, Quentin cannot break the bonds of his own virginity, even on the advice of his father:

> you are still blind to what is in yourself to that part of general truth the sequence of natural events and their causes which shadows every mans brow even Benjys you are not thinking of finitude you are contemplating an apotheosis in which a emporary state of mind will become symmetrical above the flesh and aware both of itself and of the flesh[5]

To Quentin, Caddy is a devastating force, constantly on his mind, her images surfacing and resurfacing, even drawing him into a re-enactment of a humiliating fight he had with one of her lovers. Quentin withdraws so completely from Caddy's genitive force that death is the only step remaining for him.

Jason has a dual role as he personifies 'everyman', the man of no particular talents who is trapped in a commercial world; and his is the Achilles of the novel, the angry man who must act after others fail. Characteristic of most of mankind, he is hard working, unimaginative, sentimental only in his attitude toward his mother, and inspired chiefly by a desire to get rich investing in the cotton market. Unmarried, he distrusts women:

---

3. Ibid., p. 411
4. Ibid., p. 144
5. Ibid., p. 220

> I never promise a woman anything nor let her know what I'm going to give her. That's the only way to manage them. Always keep them guessing. If you can't think of any other way to surprise them, give them a bust in the jaw.[6]

When we realize that Jason has assumed the care of Caddy's daughter, Quentin, and his mother, plus 'a whole damn kitchen full of niggers' we suspect bombast in his talk. There is a grotesque element in Jason, a harsh rejection of decency that makes him unnecessarily villainous with Caddy and the young Quentin. His unnatural, constant belligerence and occasional violent headaches suggest an imbalance in Jason. He was the 'different' child, the one not really a 'Compson' and had good reason to be jealous of Caddy and Quentin, perhaps was even shut out by the special attention given to Benjy. Still in school when Caddy brought her baby home, he was very aware of the unhappiness she caused Mrs. Compson, who turned to Jason as 'her only comfort'. Victimized by the distortions of Caddy he rejects all that she represents. This is Jason's tragedy.

What does Caddy represent, what archetype? We believe that she is beautiful long before we read it in the final pages of the novel, the 'cold beautiful face'. (It has taken the mass murderers of the Third Reich to give us a *cold* Caddy.) She moves and acts with the poise of a beautiful child, and it is as a child that we know most about her as if Faulkner wants us to see her incorrupt, in her purest, simplest form. It is not a woods nymph he gives us but an uninhibited serene being, harmonious with and complementing the lush natural greenery of the South. The 'dirty drawers' episode has been fully interpreted, and it is valid as symbolic of Caddy's future; but it is inadequate as a thesis for the book as it is the 'tomboy' that appeals to us, the free spirit refusing to be hampered by the rules her brothers respect. Faulkner has told us that for him the novel began here; for the reader it is 'here' that we know we are reading a love story.

But how do we reconcile this vibrant little female with the 'Once a bitch, always a bitch' of Jason's world? Is Faulkner ambiguous about sex? Is he preaching a gospel of promiscuity or of atonement? There is an apt link with antiquity through Jason III, Faulkner's philosophic voice:

> James III (bred for a lawyer and indeed he kept an office upstairs above the Square, where entombed in dusty filing-cases some of the oldest names in the county—Holston and Sutpen, Grenier and Beauchamp and Coldfield—faded year by year among the bottomless labyrinths of chancery...)

---

6. Ibid., p. 240

sat all day long with a decanter of whiskey and a litter of dogeared Horaces and Liveys and Catulluses, composing (it was said) caustic and satiric eulogies on both his dead and living fellowtownsmen...[7]

Of all the family Jason III is least disturbed about Caddy's behavior, and he tries to relieve Quentin's anguish:

"you wanted to sublimate a piece of natural human folly into a horror and to exorcise it with truth"

Women are never virgins. Purity is a negative state and therefore contrary to nature. It's nature is hurting you not Caddy and I said That's just words and he said So is virginity and I said you don't know. You can't know and he said Yes. (On the instant when we come to realize that tragedy is second-hand.)[8]

So Faulkner is not talking about atonement for sin, rather a positive, natural, human folly—'what is in yourself...general truth'. Caddy's words are:

the swing the cedars the secret surges the breathing locked the wild breath the yes yes yes....When they touched me I died.[9]

She loves Quentin, but she will not deny herself:

she held my hand against her chest her heart thudding I turned and caught her arm
Caddy you hate him dont you
she moved my hand up against her throat her heart was hammering there
poor Quentin
yes I hate him I would die for him I've already died for him I die for him over and over again every time.[10]

Caddy's archetype is Biblical Eve who was told at the Fall that henceforth she would bear her children in pain. Genetically, woman accepts pain as part of the greater gift of life giving, and she is very secure in this role; she is endowed with an innate toughness and a stubbornness of spirit. Genetically, it is man's fate to

---

7. Ibid., p. 409–410
8. Ibid., p. 143
9. Ibid., p. 185
10. Ibid., p. 187–188

struggle against a spiritual vacuum; he is in constant pursuit of ideals, the genetic grail-chaser. Man is the aesthete who needs beauty and whose spiritual insecurity demands exclusive rights to what he achieves—a pristine beauty. So woman's virginity is vital to man's belief in himself, and moral codes originate with him. Not personally needing a defined moral system Genetic Woman is unreasonable and illogical when she uses it to protect those she loves. Jason III explains Mrs. Compson's behavior with Caddy:

> Women only use other people's codes of honour.[11]

> Women are like that they dont acquire knowledge of people we are for that they are just born with a practical fertility of suspicion that makes a crop every so often and usually right they have an affinity for evil for supplying whatever the evil lacks in itself for drawing it about them instinctively as you do bedclothing in slumber fertilizing the mind for it until the evil has served its purpose whether it ever existed or no[12]

It is with 'other people's codes of honour' that woman short-sightedly distorts morality into tragedy as Mrs. Compson surely does with a daughter and a son and a granddaughter; she creates the 'second-hand' tragedy, the archetypal folly of chivalry, the culture of the South before the war. The society that enslaved others denied itself of its own humanity. Her role of pampered woman denied Mrs. Compson expression of her genetic spiritual strength, and she atrophied into an ineffective hypochondriac. Her legacy to her children was a warped morality, a distorted code of behavior based on race, on bloodline, on good family name. Quentin remembers her saying:

> Why wont you bring him to the house Caddy? Why must you do like nigger women do in the pasture the ditches[13]

Are we to assume that the correctness of the action lay in the place—that a Southern gentleman's bedroom was all that was lacking? Was it his mother's spiritual frustration that warped Quentin? He slaps Caddy when he learns she has kissed 'some damn town squirt'. Was it the 'who' she kissed that started

---

11. Ibid., p. 217.
12. Ibid., p.119
13. Ibid., p. 113

him on his tragic path of emotional sterility, the Compson family pride which denied him his own humanity?

There is a direct line from Mrs. Compson's fawning helplessness to Jason's monsterish overprotection of his mother, her 'pastures' and 'ditches' that became his:

> Do you think I can afford to have her (Quentin) running about the streets with every drummer that comes to town, I say, and them telling the new ones up and down the road where to pick up a hot one when they made Jefferson[14].

It was an atrophied motherhood that was the void in which Caddy's promiscuity developed and in which Caddy became evil to Jason. From his mother Jason learned to hate women.

The difficulty in determining Faulkner's attitude on sex lies in his style of writing. We become so accustomed to following his threads of thought and his broken pieces of narrative that we fail to recognize the direct statement. He says virginity is a negative state, and he means exactly that. By 'negative' he means a retreat into non-life or death, and proceeds to illustrate this thesis with Quentin's tragic story. Faulkner frequently uses a parallel narrative that may restate his thesis or disclose it by antithesis. In this novel Benjy's non-life parallels Quentin's, and the wise variance in the intellectual abilities of the two men strengthens Faulkner's argument.

The thesis for his attitude on promiscuity began with Helen serenely living with either man; again Faulkner makes a direct statement. He chooses for his heroine a beautiful, extremely appealing woman who personifies promiscuity. With masterful writing Faulkner literally cuts through the layers of our sophistication and bias and we fall in love with a little primitive; he puts us face to face with the basic heartthrob of life. Tragic as her story is, Caddy reveals Faulkner as one of the most optimistic of twentieth-century writers. Caddy will not be denied; moral codes will neither hinder nor stop her; she may suffer, but she stubbornly functions as a woman. Faulkner again uses a parallel to emphasize and restate his thesis. Dilsey is the enduring genitive strength of woman; it is her realism that frightens Jason, and he fights her rather than risk facing the artificiality of his mother. Dilsey too, makes her emotional mark on us.

---

14. Ibid., p. 286

> she continued to weep, unmindful of the talk....Dilsey made no sound, her face did not quiver as the tears took their sunken and devious courses, walking with her head up, making no effort to dry them away even.
> "Whyn't you quit, dat, mammy?" Frony said.... "I've seed de first en de last," Dilsey said. "Never you mind me...I seed de beginning, en now I sees de endin." [15]

Faulkner is not a public moralist; he is more the diagnostician, exploring the sources of tragedy in life. Caddy Compson is love, the genetic truth of womanhood, life strength; immorality lies in her distorted roles, a theme used over and over by Faulkner; he gives us a Thomas Sutpen with a Helen-the-trophy in the house and a black Briseis in the field; a frenzied grail-chasing Joe Christmas destroying life in direct opposition to serene little Lena Grove producing life.

Faulkner's maturity as a writer may be best seen if we compare him with his contemporaries. Hemingway is a lesser writer because he fails to acknowledge woman's true nature. An eloquent spokesman for the male spiritual odyssey, Hemingway assumes the masculine insecurity for his female characters, thus limiting the scope of his writings to the Achillean challenge. Fitzgerald keeps his writing embroiled in the problems of the male ego, and his women characters are seen in adjunct to the role of the man, giving them a shallowness, lacking an identity of their own; we feel that Fitzgerald's female characters are maneuvered. Faulkner's insight gives us both a Gavin Steven's "worse than that I am only a man" and a Quentin Compson's "honour precariously and only temporarily supported by the minute fragile membrane". It is his acknowledgement of woman's superior spiritual strength that gives Faulkner's writing artistic poise and validity; he respects both her primitive strength and her sophisticated contrariness. To those of us who share D. H. Lawrence's astonishment in realizing that that paragon of virtue, Hester, might be that 'bitch in the grass', Faulkner says, "she is both, love her."

---

15. Ibid., p. 371

BIBLIOGRAPHY

Faulkner, William, *The Sound and the Fury*. Vintage Books 1946

Will Kennicott of Main Street

Dr. Will Kennicott of Sinclair Lewis' *Main Street* impresses the reader alternately as a demi-god and as a clod. The novel is a history of seven years of the marriage of Dr. Kennicott and Carol Wilford, a woman of taste and education, who encounters many problems trying to develop a home and a marriage in a young, somewhat primitive prairie town. Lewis' development of Carol's story is richly satisfying to readers; he entertains us, shares with us his own sympathetic insight into the life of a woman, and is in no way illogical in the development of her character. With Will Kennicott, however, we are occasionally jarred; we sense an inconsistency in what Lewis tells us of the doctor, and we are not sure whether we love or despise him.

Was this double-image in a character an error on the part of Lewis? Did he in some way, in order to develop his plot, try to blend the characteristics of two types of men, finding that he needed a man of the prestige of a medical doctor to lure Carol to Gopher Prairie but also needed a small-town hick to give added depth to Carol's problems? Lewis' skill as a writer and his close association with doctors in his own family make this conclusion improbable. This paper suggests that the source of the ambivalent feeling the reader has for Dr. Will Kennicott lies in a fictional concept in the reader's own mind, that the romantic idea that Americans have of the family doctor blinds us to the possibility that rather than *create* a character, Lewis presented a prototype of a man he knew intimately.

Both versions of Dr. Will's personality are believable, but we have difficulty seeing them as attributes of one man. How delightfully we respond to the heroic doctor who:

went out, hungry, chilly unprotesting; and she, before she fell asleep again, loved him for his sturdiness, and saw the drama of his riding by night to the frightened household on the distant farm...[1]

and to the Will Kennicott who, "speaks a vulgar, common, incorrect German of life and death and birth and the soil".[2] How wise this prairie psychologist seems to us when he says to his patient Maud Dyer:

> As a matter of fact, you're right. You have a perfectly well-developed case of repression of sex instinct, and it raises the old Ned with your body. What you need is to get away from Dave and travel, yes, and go to every dog-gone kind of New Thought and Bahai and Swami and Hooptedoodle meeting you can find. I know it, well's you do. But how can I advise it? Dave would be up here taking my hide off. I'm willing to be family physician and priest and lawyer and plumber and wet-nurse, but I draw the line at making Dave loosen up on money. Too hard a job in weather like this! So, savvy, my dear? Believe it will rain if this heat keeps...[3]

And how we admire and love him for his understanding and kindness when his skittish wife is indiscreet in her relations with the young Eric Valborg:

> Wait now, don't get sore! I'm not knocking him. He isn't a bad sort. And he's young and likes to gas about books. Course you like him. That isn't the real rub.[4]

This is the country doctor that America knows and loves; this is the family doctor of everyone's childhood—the giant among men whose learning and goodness symbolized authority with love—the outlet for the emotionally 'king'-starved European immigrant who was not even sure what democracy meant. This is the man who established a tradition in the American home, a tradition that placed the doctor just a little below God.

But in *Main Street* Lewis insists that the country doctor was mortal, and prosaic, and fumbling, even crude, that he could chew tobacco and "spit" in the living room:

---

1. Sinclair Lewis, *Main Street*, (New York: Harcourt, Brace and Company, 1921), p. 177
2. Ibid., p. 192
3. Ibid., p. 309
4. Ibid., p. 396

> And God knows I want to be fair. But I expect others to be fair too. And you're so high and mighty about people. Take Sam Clark; best soul that ever lived, honest and loyal and a damn good fellow…Sam drops around in the evening to sit and visit, and by golly just because he takes a dry smoke and rolls his cigar around in his mouth, and maybe spits a few times, you look at him as if he was a hog. Oh, you didn't know I was onto you, and I certainly hope Sam hasn't noticed it, but I never miss it.[5]

It is hard for Americans to visualize a medical demi-god.

> …reduced to humility…stirred to rise from the table, and to hold the chair for her; and all through supper he ate his bread dry because he felt that she would think him common if he said "Will you hand me the butter?"[6]

We reluctantly lose our vision of the "dedicated healer" in the man who fusses with the draft on the furnace and the price of farmland. We are dismayed with the doctor who lacks insight, who could live with a woman for five years and never think to question what part he might have had in changing a woman from a bride who was "surprised at how tumultuous a feeling could be roused in her"[7] to a woman he calls "cold" six years later.

The ambivalence in the characterization of Will Kennicott surely lies in our own stereotyped thinking. We cannot believe that the sacred title of "Doctor" could be given to a man who at heart will remain a hayseed all of his life, nor can we imagine that at the same age Will Kennicott may have been distressingly like Cy Bogart. How much could a medical education do to develop a raw-boned prairie boy into a sensitive man? For generations the course of study in our medical schools has been a demanding and grueling training in the physical sciences with time only to develop authority and conscience in these students. Effective training in the humanities was unknown for the men of Will Kennicott's day, nor would it be much different for the doctor's grandson if he were a medical student at the University of Minnesota today.

Perhaps our disenchantment with Will Kennicott derives from a romantic notion of the practice of medicine, generally. The work is physically exhausting but so emotionally satisfying that a doctor's chief needs at home may be merely food and a bed. Thus, his new house may be the trophy of financial success, the

---

5. Ibid., p. 171.
6. Ibid., p. 74.
7. Ibid., p. 22.

new car every year both a status symbol and a toy, the affair with another woman the privilege of a demi-god, and his wife only a functional being to raise his family. It is to be wondered that all men of Kennicott's profession do not automatically become household beasts!

Carol Kennicott was beaten in her attempts to make her marriage and her life in Gopher Prairie meaningful and satisfying. But her husband did not defeat her; she was undone by that age-old enemy of all of women's efforts to improve their state in life, the whore. Maud Dyer completely disarmed Carol and deprived her of the one sure weapon she had with which to provoke a vital confrontation with Will Kennicott. The tragedy is that in their minor skirmishes over money and a new house Will Kennicott did change; he learned, and he conceded. But there was nothing in Carol Kennicott's background to alert her to the possibility of immorality.

In his characterization of Will Kennicott Lewis challenges us to look through the clouds of our own romantic delusions and see in the country doctor something of every man, and see that, although Will Kennicott is a clod, a country bumpkin, he is an admirable professional man; and an eloquent one in a hackneyed way:

> Carrie do you understand my work?...No matter if you are cold, I like you better than anybody in the world. One time I said that you were my soul. And that still goes...Do you realize what my job is? I go round twenty-four hours a day, in mud and blizzard, trying my damnedest to heal everybody, rich or poor. You—that're always spieling about how scientists ought to rule the world, instead of a bunch of spread-eagle politicians—can't you see that I'm all the science there is here? And I can stand the cold and the bumpy roads and the lonely rides at night. All I need is to have you here at home to welcome me. I don't expect you to be passionate—not any more I don't—but I do expect you to appreciate my work. I bring babies into the world, and save lives and make cranky husbands quit being mean to their wives. And then you go and moon over a Swede tailor because he can talk about how to put ruchings on a skirt! Hell of a thing for a man to fuss over![8]

8.　Ibid., p. 396

BIBLIOGRAPHY

Lewis, Sinclair, *Main Street.* New York: Harcourt, Brace and Company, 1921

Christopher Marlowe, A Renaissance Poet

"Men of the Renaissance, like their Greek and Roman kinsmen, glorified the human form as a thing of beauty and the human intellect as capable of discovering all truth worth knowing."[1] Harrison and Sullivan make the above statement in a history on western civilization, listing various political, religious, and artistic leaders who epitomized the spirit of the Renaissance in several countries of Europe, and they include the name of Christopher Marlowe as one who particularly exemplified the English Renaissance. In this paper I hope to discover and isolate the words of Marlowe which earned a young poet historical recognition and to determine what contribution he may have made as a Renaissance poet.

A formal education to the degree of Master of Arts must have been a rare privilege in the sixteenth-century world. Christopher Marlowe had that privilege, chiefly because he was born in Canterbury, a city where his particular aptitude for intellectual development would be recognized and where beneficent church authorities could make a scholarship to Cambridge University available to him. The purpose of this scholarship was to train ministers for the Anglican Church, but Marlowe was able to reject this vocation with little or no retributive action from the school administration;[2] and in justice to the poet I must admit that I found no evidence of criticism of the Anglican Church in his writings. It seems somewhat ironic to me, however, that a man who benefited

---

1. John B. Harrison and Richard E. Sullivan, *A Short History of Western Civilization*, Allfred A. Knopf, Inc., New York, 1966, p. 343
2. John Bakeless, *Christopher Marlowe, The Man in His Time*, William Morrow and Company, New York, 1937, p. 73

so much from a system of education could so bitterly attack the administration of the Roman Catholic Church which had maintained and advanced formal learning throughout its history. Admittedly, the medieval Christian theologians governed their schools by the philosophy that man and his intellect are frail, prone to pride, and in constant need of Christian inspiration to perceive truth; and this did result in a rigidly disciplined system of education, stifling free inquiry which is still regarded as a necessary attribute to the pursuit of learning. But Marlowe did not experience this suppression; the evidence is that he was a brilliant student, not always faithful in attendance but with no record of overt rebelliousness to the discipline of the school. The fact is that in his time he was a well-educated man, a commoner with an advanced educational degree, truly representative of Renaissance achievement. We can only guess that it was this new spirit of freedom plus Marlowe's intense English patriotism that engendered his distrust of the Roman Church.

The most obvious result of Marlowe's learning is manifested in the early sources of his plays. It is difficult to date the plays of Marlowe because English writers at this time were not concerned with getting their manuscripts printed. Ben Jonson was the first writer of this time to collect his writings in a folio, and was regarded as vainly pretentious for doing so.[3] Rather than seeking fame through print Marlowe and his contemporaries gave their works to friends for reading, or in the case of dramas sold them to play houses or acting companies. This has made it difficult to determine just when a play was written as it was not printed while it was still popular on the stage. *Tamburlaine* was the only one of his plays that was printed in Marlowe's lifetime.[4] Tucker Brooke believes that both *Tamburlaine* and *Dido* were written while Marlowe was still a student at Cambridge;[5] it was his university training that provided Marlowe with source material for his plots, *Dido* being based on the first, second and fourth books of the *Aeneid* and *Tamburlaine* based on his own research into the life of a fourteenth century Mongolian Khan Timur. Modern scholars are impressed with the amount of reading that Marlowe must have done to have written this play as they can find sources of it in the writing of the Spaniard Mexia, the Italian Perondinus, the German Lonicerus, and an Italian Bishop

---

3. Bakeless, p. 309
4. Bakeless, p. 308
5. C.F. Tucker Brooke, ed., *The Works and Life of Christopher Marlowe, The Life of Marlowe and the Tragedy of Dido Queen of Carthage*, R.H. Case, general editor, Goridan Press Inc., New York, 1966, pp. 115–119.

Jovius. In addition to these writings as sources for *Tamburlaine* scholars are certain that Marlowe consulted Paul Ive's *Practise of Fortification* for descriptions of battle scenes and the maps of Ortelius for the geography.[6] The dramatization of *The Tragical History of Doctor Faustus* is based entirely upon a translation in English of a German work *Historia von D Johann Fausten* published at Frankfort-on-the-Main. For *The Jew of Malta* Marlowe probably read a collection of chronicles on Turkish affairs written by Philip Lonecirus containing the story of a Portugese Jew, Jan Miques.[7] Tucker Brooke believes that Marlowe knew of David Passi, a Jew of Constantinople, from stories told to him by Sir Walter Raliegh and the Walsinghams.[8] In his last play Marlowe turned to Holinshed's *Chronicles* for the story of Edward II. Scholars try to date these plays definitely because it is interesting to know which playwright may have innovated a new form first, in this case the history play. Some scholars believe that *Edward II* was written in 1591 and Shakespeare's *2 and 3 Henry VI* in 1592.[9] Charlton and Waller believe that *Henry VI* was the earlier play;[10] whatever the truth the evidence is that the two dramatists knew each other at this time, and shows us that Marlowe was still the student turning to books for source material. Bennett says that researchers are impressed at the scope of sources for Marlowe's play, particularly *Tamburlaine* and *Massacre at Paris*, and at his ability to use many sources to write a play which proved to be historically true even though the source material was incomplete or inaccurate.[11]

Harrison and Sullivan characterize the Renaissance man as 'versatile'.[12] Marlowe's writings attest to his versatile interests. There are many geographical references in his plays; *Tamburlaine* is filled with references to Asian kingdoms, allusions he used both to excite the imagination of the theatergoer and

---

6. Bakeless, p. 122.
7. H.S. Bennett, ed., *The Works and Life of Christopher Marlowe, The Jew of Malta and The Massacre at Paris*, R.H. Case, general editor, Gordian Press Inc., New York, 1966, p. 10
8. Bennett, p. 11
9. G.B. Harrison, ed., *Shakespeare, the Complete Works*, Harcourt, Brace and World, Inc., New York, 1968, p. 103.
10. H.B. Carlton and R.D. Waller, eds., *The Works and Life of Christopher Marlowe, Edward II*, R.H. Case, general editor, Gordian Press, Inc., New York, 1966, p. 25.
11. Bennett, p. 5
12. Harrison and Sullivan, p. 344.

to contribute to the music of his poetry.[13] We know that Marlowe traveled on the continent, even working as a spy for the British government in 1587, and Bennett states that Marlowe had an 'intimate connection' with the 'underworld of Elizabethan politics'.[14] The sources of The Massacre at Paris are those of an active, versatile man; we know that books and pamphlets describing the civil wars in France were available to him and that Marlowe visited France several times;[15] in addition to this there were Protestant refugees from France known to people in England, and Marlowe certainly knew of them.[16] Within the context of his plays there are references to scientific thought of the day indicating that Marlowe had a student's or a man-of-affair's interest in activities other than literary. In Faustus we have the knowledge-seeking doctor questioning Mephistopheles about the plan of the universe; Mephistopheles says the world is 'centric'. Tamburlaine says that man is composed of 'four elements', 'part of the plan of nature' suggesting Marlowe's belief in the philosophy of Plato. In Tamburlaine there are two references to the veins and arteries in the human body; William Harvey, a man of Marlowe's generation, defined the human circulatory system.

Christopher Marlowe was a good student of classical mythology, the play Dido demonstrates this as does his unfinished poem Hero and Leander. It is difficult for me to make a judgment on just how much Marlowe accepted Latin or Greek philosophy as I am not familiar with the study of philosophy and would not recognize such sources in his thinking. But he made much use of mythology in his writings as a source for terms descriptive of emotional experiences; the mythology is like a new English for him, a new dimension in his language for descriptions of beauty and pleasure. The whole sensuous experience of Hero and Leander is framed by the sexual adventures of gods; Marlowe resurrects Helen of Troy as the ultimate woman in Faustus. Tamburlaine is like a demi-god whose exploits can be ended only by death; all through this play there is an epic spirit, an aura of the classical epics.

It is easy to show Marlowe as a man of the new learning, a versatile sixteenth-century man, but Harrington and Sullivan further describe the Renaissance man as 'secular', and the secular attitude as characterized by 'Humanism',

---

13. Bakeless, p. 274
14. Bennett, p. 187.
15. Bakeless, p. 177.
16. Ibid., P.248

or the making of man, not God the chief center of interest in life.[17] The break with Rome by Henry VIII in England and Luther in Germany and by others on the continent upset an order—the traditional power of the Church of Rome was broken. Now man's efforts could be directed in ways other than that of the promotion of the life of the Church. Governments had divorced themselves from Rome's control; national thinking was directed toward world exploration and rising commercialism; and in the universities men were free to pursue knowledge for its intriguing intellectualism and its aesthetic pleasure. To what extent are Marlowe's writings the products of a secular philosophy? How successfully does he put man in 'center-stage' without the trappings of a religious discipline?

Exposure of hypocrisy has a universal appeal, as man seems to love both fair play and witch-hunting; we respond to exposure of devious behavior in others in a positive way—it attracts us, and Marlowe used it to make good theatre. Marlowe wrote little comedy, but he was adroit in satire, and the religious hypocrite is found in much of his drama. Most frequently the pagan or the non-Christian character exposes religious insincerity in Christian characters. The Turkish King Orcanes says in *Tamburlaine II*:

> Can there be such deceit in Christians,
> II, ii, 36

and

> Then, if there be a Christ, as Christians say,
> But in their deeds deny him for their Christ.
> II, ii, 38–40

In *The Jew of Malta* Christian hypocrisy seems almost the paramount theme; Jews are the cursed race, the infidels, but there is a severe judgment of Christian behavior. Barabas says:

> Rather had I, a Jew, be hated thus
> Than pitied in a Christian poverty:
> Nor can I see no fruits in all their faith,
> But malice, falsehood, and excessive pride.
> I, I, 112–115

---

17. Harrison and Sullivan, p.343

> Is theft the ground of your religion?
> I, ii, 96

Ferneze, the Christian governor, tells Barabas:

> No, Jew....
> But here in Malta, where thou gotts't thy wealth,
> Live still; and if thou canst, get more.
> I, ii, 103–104

Barabas counsels his daughter Abigail:

> Ay, daughter; for religion
> Hides many mischiefs from suspicion.
> I, ii, 280–281

When she knows that she is dying Abigail talks to Friar Jacomo:

> ah, gentle friar,
> Convert my father that he may be sav'd,
> And witness that I die a Christian!
> Friar: Ay, an a virgin too; that grieves me most.
> III, vi, 38–41

Marlowe makes many statements criticizing the Pope through other characters, but in *Faustus* the Pope condemns himself:

> To me and Peter shalt thou groveling lie,
> And crouch before the Papal dignity.
> III, i, 95–96

> Adding this golden sentence to our praise:—
> "That Peter's heirs should tread on Emperors,
> III, i, 139–140

In *The Massacre at Paris* the Catholic Duke Guise is scheming to gain control of the throne of France, knowing that he has the support of the Catholic factions; Conde, one of the peers, says of Guise:

> My lord, you need not marvel at the Guise,
> For what he doth, the Pope will ratify,
> In murder, mischief, or in tyranny.
> > Scene I, 181–183

It is tempting to believe that rather than vilify the Church Marlowe is subtly suggesting that she is merely temporarily corrupt, that he is directing his satire on the villainous who operate within the structure of the Church. But this is not true; in all of Marlowe's plays there is only one character who receives comfort from the Church, Abigail. Ironically, the playwright has her turning to Christianity less for spiritual comfort than for a physical haven; we feel that after the murder of her lover through the scheming of her father there is no other place for her to go.

The Roman Catholic Church regards life as a preparation for life after death; perhaps the Church is over-zealous in her concern with death, but she is realistic in her belief that the spiritually weak suffer at the thought of death. For this reason I was particularly interested in the way that Marlowe's characters faced their own death. I found a consistently secular attitude in these scenes. Marlowe's death scenes are like super-charged confrontations with the powers of after-life. In the seven plays there are only two natural deaths, Zenocrate and Tamburlaine. Tamburlaine's grief for Zenocrate is eloquent, but he believes that she lives on, that Jove has stolen her—the gods have affronted the power of Tamburlaine the Great:

> Batter the shining palace of the sun,
> And shiver all the starry firmament,
> For amorous Jove hath snatched my love from hence,
> Meaning to make her stately queen of heaven.
> What god soever holds thee in his arms,
> Giving thee nectar and ambrosia,
> Behold me, here, divine Zenocrate,
> Raving, impatient, desperate and mad.
> > *Tamburlaine II,* II, iv, 105–112

Tamburlaine has a positive view of his own death—he is immortal:

> But son, this subject, not of force enough
> To hold the fiery spirit it contains,
> Must part, imparting his impressions
> My equal portions into both your breasts;

> My flesh, divided in your precious shapes,
> Shall still retain my spirit, though I die
> And live in all your seeds immortally.
> *Tamburlaine II*, V, iii, 168-173

The Jew of Malta dies unrepentant:

> Then, Barabas, breathe forth thy latest fate,
> And in the fury of thy torments, strive
> To end thy life with resolution:
> V, v, 78–80
> Die, life! fly, soul! tongue, curse thy fill, and die!
> V, v, 89

Faustus knows only too well what death means for him—Mephistopheles made that clear—and of all the death scenes this is the most dramatic. To me, Faustus is hypocritical; certainly he is frightened; his prayers to the Christian god are eloquent and impassioned, but he cowardly grasps for comfort in pagan beliefs:

> Ah, Pythagoras' *metempsychosis*, were that true,
> This soul should fly from me, and I be changed
> Unto some brutish beast; all beasts are happy,
> For, when they die
> Their souls are soon dissolved in elements.
> V, ii, 178–182

Three of Marlowe's characters die crying for revenge; Dido seeks revenge on Aenaes with her suicide, and the Duke of Guise and Edward die calling for revenge for their murders. Guise alone is humiliated:

> To die by peasants, what a grief is this!
> Scene XVIII, 180

Marlowe's characters face death alone, no one calls for the clergy or looks to another character for spiritual comfort. There are not many situations in these plays where one could examine a character's response to crisis other than in the death scenes, as the action of the plays, particularly in the earlier ones, is always a strong forward motion toward a well-defined goal. The poet never deals with fate or prophecy. Good and bad angels appear in *Faustus*, but they are more like a debating team than supernatural beings; Faustus' fate was the result of his own intellectual decision. Marlowe's characters draw their strength from the heavens, the stars, the scope of the universe. Even treacherous Guise says:

> What glory is there in a common good,
> That hanges for every peasant to atchiue?
> That like I best that flyes beyond my reach.
> Set me to scale the high Pyramides,
> And thereon set the Diadem of Fraunce,
> Ile either rend it with my nayles to naught,
> Or mount the top with my aspiring winges,
> Although my downfall be the deepest hell.
> For this, I wake, when others think I sleepe,
> For this, I waite, that scornes attendance else.
> *The Massacre at Paris*, Scene II, 40–49

What did Marlowe, the complete Renaissance man, contribute to English literature? He wrote both poetry and drama, but since pastoral poetry has never appealed to me I hesitate to make a judgment on his pastoral poetry; he could write this lyric poetry both in simple English terms and in a language filled with classical allusions. I do, however, recognize the development of Marlowe as a dramatist. Bakeless briefly traces the history of the drama, giving us some perspective on the theater of Marlowe's time.

> Blank verse reached the practical, commercial stage one day in 1587 or 1588, when young Christopher Marlowe walked into the Theatre or the Curtain with the manuscript of *Tamburlaine* under his arm. It is not certain...that his play was the first blank verse to astonish the ears of the groundlings....*The Spanish Tragedie*....written by Thomas Kyd may have preceded it on the stage....This was 'Marlowe's mighty line', and no matter how clumsily it was imitated, no matter how much it was ridiculed and parodied...it brought to the English stage for the first time 'the heady music of the five marching lambs',[18] ...Marlowe's *Tamburlaine* is an early example of a kind of play common enough in Elizabethan days. It is neither tragedy nor comedy, but a chronicle play, based on more or less authentic history, re-written and adapted for the stage.[19]

---

18. Bakeless, p. 108
19. Ibid, p. 110.

Significant improvement in Marlowe's dramatic technique is obvious if we compare his first play with his last. *Tamburlaine I*, the earliest play, has little real plot: a shepherd becomes a world conqueror by a series of military triumphs through many exotic-sounding countries; at the end he very grandly marries the woman he had captured and made his concubine. Rather than plot or character development we have a succession of brutal war episodes, the magic of the play lying in the poetry and the theatricalism. The Tamburlaine at the end of the play is no different from the one at the beginning. His love for Zenocrate is passionate and divine, but it became so very abruptly. In *Tamburlaine II* three sons appear and both Zenocrate and Tamburlaine die; the war episodes vary, but there is little change in structure from *Tamburlaine I*.

Edward II has a firm plot; it is the story of a weak king who loses his crown and his life because of that weakness. The play is based on the life of Edward II of England (1310-1330) and the people who supported or opposed him. Marlowe handles this drama with a degree of polish although the action of the play lacks good timing; Gaveston goes to Ireland and back about as fast as Abigail entered and left the nunnery in *The Jew of Malta*. The characters involved in the plots against the king are not distinct; Kent and Spencer are confusing although Kent is brother to Edward. The story of Gaveston is an effective subplot, but we are not sure whether Gaveston is good or evil. He is presented as a lover of the king, possible destroyer of Queen Isabella's marriage, but he is a lover of Isabella too. Within a few lines we learn that Gaveston loves the king's niece, and he does marry her with the king rejoicing over the marriage. Gaveston's personality is confusing to the reader, and we do not regret his death in the middle of the play. Mortimer Junior is a believable character, Queen Isabella less so. Prince Edward changes from a child to a king very quickly. There is suspense in the play as Edward is a sympathetic character, and until the last act we rather hope that he may triumph over the peers.

One important difference between *Edward II* and *Tamburlaine* is that Marlowe deals with realism in this play. The king is not invincible, and he must face intrigue and forces stronger and more idealistic than he is. References are made to the burdens of the throne. An important element in this play is a gradually developing definition of government for the secular man. It is as if Marlowe is now acknowledging the need for order in men's lives, the need for a special leadership. Gaveston is disliked because he is 'not a gentleman'; Warwick tells the king:

You that are princely-born should shake him off.
  I, iv, 80

Mortimer Junior wants a king to 'seem glorious to the world', and the Bishop of Winchester asks Edward to surrender his crown 'for England's good'.

Other differences in this play from the earlier one is the use of speech-like passages—stichomythia, few soliloquies and no extremely long speeches. There is less brutality as only Edward is murdered on stage. I do not believe that the poetry of *Edward II* is better than that of *Tamburlaine*, but certainly the differences in the two plays represent the development of a potentially great dramatist.

It has been so easy for me to apply the Harrington-Sullivan definition of the Renaissance man to the life and writings of Christopher Marlowe that it is almost as if they studied the man and then wrote the definition. I do not see Marlowe as a contemplative; his poetry is uninhibited in style with a cadence well-suited to characters seeking the ultimate experience, people so enraptured with the scope of their own being that they are passionately involved with living, never hesitating, never unsure of themselves. In his last two plays Marlowe has these amoral forces meeting and clashing, but he died before his dramatic sense demanded of him that he deal with the inner man, the man who makes moral judgments on himself. Marlowe was born into an exciting period in history, and he responded to its challenges with a love for life, for beauty, and for freedom.

BIBLIOGRAPHY

A Short History of Western Civilization, John B. Harrison and Richard E. Sullivan, Alfred A. Knopf, Inc., New York, 1966

Christopher Marlowe, The Man in His Time, John Bakeless William Morrow and Company, New York, 1937

The Renaissance, Its Nature and Origins, George Clark Sellery, The University of Wisconsin Press, Madison, 1950

Shakespeare, the Complete Works, G.B. Harrison, ed., Marcourt, Brace, and World, Inc., New York, 1968

The Works and Life of Christopher Marlowe, R.H. Case, general editor, *Edward II*, H.B. Charlton and C.D. Waller, editors, Gordian Press Inc., New York, 1966

The Works and Life of Christopher Marlowe, R.H. Case, general editor, *Marlowe's Poems*, L.C. Martin, ed., Gordian Press, Inc., New York, 1966

The Works and Life of Christopher Marlowe, R.H. Case, general editor, *Tamburlaine the Great*, U.M. Ellis-Fermor, ed., Gordian Press, Inc., New York, 1966

The Works and Life of Christopher Marlowe, R.H. Case, general editor, *The Jew of Malta and The Massacre at Paris*, H.S. Bennett, ed., Gordian Press, Inc., New York, 1966

The Works and Life of Christopher Marlowe, R.H. Case, general editor, *The Life of Marlowe and the Tragedy of Dido Queen of Carthage*, C.F. Tucker Brooke, ed., Gordian Press, Inc., New York, 1966

The Works and Life of Christopher Marlowe, R.H. Case, general editor, *The Tragical History of Doctor Faustus*, Frederick S. Boas, ed., Gordian Press, Inc., New York, 1966

A Study of The Idylls of the King

In that fierce light which beats upon a throne
And blackens every blot
Break not, O woman's-heart, but endure,
Break not, for thou art royal, but endure.

The above lines from the "Dedication" of Tennyson's *Idylls of the King* were not addressed to the tragic queen of Camelot; these lines are written here out of context, as the first two lines are part of a description of Prince Albert's blameless life, and the last two lines are addressed to the surviving Queen Victoria. To the reader, however, who is familiar with the story of Arthur and Guinevere, the lines suggest an eloquence and a depth of meaning that is lost when the poetry alludes to Albert and Victoria: the nineteenth century rulers are intrusive. This juxtaposition of the four English monarchs overshadows the whole poem, as the throne of England is central to its thesis. Tennyson designed the poem this way; whatever other changes may have occurred in his thinking during the thirty or forty years that he spent writing *The Idylls of the King*, he did not deviate from his original purpose of presenting an ideal ruler, an English monarch who exemplified the highest ideal of manhood. This ideal Tennyson attributed to Prince Albert and presented through the character of King Arthur. Tennyson dedicated the poem to Albert's memory:

> a Prince indeed...Albert the Good
> These to his memory...
> I dedicate, I consecrate with tears—
> These Idylls.[1]

and he addressed the epilogue to Queen Victoria:

> —But thou, my Queen
> Not for itself, but thro' thy living love
> For one to whom I made it o'er his grave
> Sacred...(254)

We have the poet's own words for his concept of the role of King Arthur:

> "The vision of an ideal Arthur as I have drawn him," my father said, "had come upon me when little more than a boy, I first lighted upon Malory;" (My father's MS.) and it dwelt with him to the end....My father felt strongly and passionately that only under the inspiration of ideals, and with his "Sword bathed in heaven", can a man combat the cynical indifference, the intellectual selfishness, the sloth of will, the utilitarian materialism of a transition age....My father said on his eightieth birthday: "My meaning in the *Idylls of the King* was spiritual. I took the legendary stories of the Round Table as illustrations. I intended Arthur to represent the Ideal Soul of Man coming into contact with the warring elements of the flesh."[2]

The idea of King Arthur in the role of great spiritual leadership is interesting to the student of the Arthurian legend. Arthur has proved himself to be a more than adequate hero in many stages of the literary development of the English people. Starting as a conqueror of barbaric Celtic tribes in the fifth century, he easily developed into a heroic *chevalier* of feudal times, a champion of Christian doctrine for the monks of the middle ages, a worthy monarch in the dazzling courts of the fourteenth century, and always an inspiring subject for moralists. Added to his epic and heroic nature is Arthur's initiation of the

---

1. Alfred Lord Tennyson, *The Idylls of the King*, (New York: New American Library, 1961) p. 13. All quotations of the poetry will be from this book, followed by the page number in parenthesis.
2. Hallam, Lord Tennyson, ed., Alfred Lord Tennyson, *The Idylls of the King* (New York: AMS Press, 1970), pp. 443–445.

quest for the Holy Grail, which gives the weight of precedence to Tennyson's interpretation.

Tennyson succeeded in writing a great tribute to the throne of England, but the *Idylls of the King* is not a great poem in the sense of being a classic; it is not epic; it will not endure as great tragedy. The *Idylls* is parochial and ironically sentimental because Tennyson manipulated classical characters to fit Victorian modes. In his zealous support of the monarchy in England, he tried to relate fantasy to fact with the result that his portrayals of Arthur and Lancelot in particular become caricatures, too political to be allegorical, too maneuvered to be tragic. Lancelot, strongest, gentlest, and most beloved of the knights, is Tennyson's villain, an offender against the crown of England. Arthur is self-righteous, suspicious, and didactic; a man Malory would not emulate, and a complete stranger to the Wart who thought he was stealing the sword he found embedded in the stone.

The poetry of the *Idylls*, however, is beautiful; few people would disagree with Henry James' observation: "As a didactic creation, I do not greatly care for King Arthur, but as a fantastic one he is infinitely remunerative." Much of the best poetry in the poem is found in the passages where Tennyson describes Arthur, the King. From the beginning of the poem he presents an Arthur of dramatic scope; Arthur, the warrior, is a man invincible, described with images of gigantic proportions, sweeping movements, and a consistent sense of the supernatural. In the "Coming of Arthur" the young king 'drew under him petty princedoms', he 'drave the heathen, slew the beast, fell'd the forest, saw the smallest rock on faintest hill'. The lines 'From the great deep to great deep he goes', appear at least three times in the poem. In "Guinevere" Arthur is called 'mightiest', the Round Table, a 'glorious company—model for a mighty world'. He even dies in high style: 'They summon me their King to lead mine hosts/Far down to that great battle in the west.' (238) In "The Passing of Arthur" with the last battle over and Arthur dying, Tennyson sustains a sense of far-reaching power that protects the helpless king:

> The great brand
> Made lightnings in the splendor of the moon
> And flashing round and round, and whirl'd in an arch,
> Shot like a streamer of the northern morn,
> Seen where the moving isles of winter shock
> By night, with noises of the Northern Sea. (249)

With a skillful blend of the world of magic and the world of Christianity, Tennyson gives us a supernatural being, a god: 'the boundless purpose of the king', 'the fires of God descended upon him in battlefield', and 'The king stood out in heaven crown'd'. Mist appears at dramatic moments; Leodogran is debating with himself to decide whether or not Arthur is a worthy man to whom he may give his daughter, Guinevere; he finds his answer in a dream. The eerie beauty of Leodogran's dream is artistic, eminently poetic:

> Dreaming, a slope of land that ever grew
> Field after field, up to a height, the peak
> Haze-hidden, and thereon a phantom king,
> Now looming, and now lost; and on the slope
> The sword rose, the hind fell, the herd was driven
> Fire glimpsed; and all the land from roof and rick
> In drifts of smoke before a rolling wind
> Stream'd to the peak, and mingled with the haze
> And made it thicker; while the phantom king
> Sent out at times a voice, and here or there
> Stood one who pointed toward the voice, the rest
> Slew on and burnt, crying, "No king of ours,
> No son of Uther, and no king of ours;"
> Till with a wink his dream was changed, the haze
> Descended, and the solid earth became
> As nothing, but the King stood out in heaven. (24–25)

This is fantasy, extravaganza, good poetry, but far-fetched in terms of a political figure. Arthur was a successful warrior and a successful king, but his immortality lies in his humanity, in the dilemma of a man who learns that the man he loves best has stolen the affections of the woman he loves best. Arthur's humanity is a legacy from Malory:

> For, as the Frenshe book seyth, the kynge was full loathe that such a noyse shulde be upon sir Launcelot and his queen; for the kynge had a demyng of hit, but he wold nat here thereof, for sir Launcelot had done so much for hym and for the queen so many tymes that wyte you well the kynge loved hym passyngly well.[3]

---

3. Eugene Vinaver, ed., Sir Thomas Malory. *Works* (New York: Oxford University Press, 1971), p. 674.

Tennyson needed an Arthur of broader scope; he used magnificence as a literary device to broaden the seriousness of Lancelot's sin, to make it actually an offense against the throne.

The affair between Lancelot and Guinevere dates back to the beginnings of the Arthurian legend itself, when, in the middle of the sixth century, the Llancarfan Monk Gildas, wrote of the exploits of an early English king who ruled the Celtic people during the last part of the fifth century.[4] In 1130 Carodoc, also a Welch monk, wrote a *Life of St. Gildas*, which contains an incident that is an early form of the story of Lancelot and Guinevere.[5] The story of the knight's love for the queen is found in the writings of the French Monk Chretien de Troyes, of the twelfth century, and in the romances of the French Vulgate Cycle of the lance fifteenth century.[6]

In the long literary tradition of the story of the Round Table Lancelot is a transgressor, but he is ever the ideal knight, the epitome of chivalry, worthy of the love of a queen and noble in his love for Guinevere, as she is the only woman to whom he ever gives himself willingly. We love the Lancelot of Malory's "A Noble Tale of Sir Launcelot du Lake":

> So this sir Launcelot encresed mervaylously in worship and honoure; therefore he is the first knight that the Frey(n)sh booke makyth me(n)cion of aftir kynge Arthure com frome Rome. Wherefore, queen Gwenyvere had hym in grete favoure aboven all other knghtis, and so he loved the queen agayne aboven all other ladyes dayes of his lyff, and for her he dud many dedys of armys and saved her frome the fyre thorow his noble chivalry.[7]
> ....And so at that tyme sir Launcelot had the grettyste name of ony knight of the worlde, and moste he was honoured of hyghe and lowe.[8]

The whole poem is episodic, following generally the same pattern of episodes that Malory did: the knights are emissaries of the court who go into the countryside to bring justice and law to the populace and then return to tell of their experiences to King Arthur and the members of the Round Table. Arthur is central to the legend, unifying the stories and giving them continuity; Tennyson adds a second unifying device—'the world's loud whisper', the sin of

---

4. Richard Barber, *King Arthur* (Ipswich: The Boydell Press, 1974) p. 14.
5. *Ibid*, p. 16.
6. *Ibid*, p. 81
7. *Ibid*, p. 149
8. Malory, p. 175.

Lancelot. There is a sketchy plot that combines the spread of the knowledge of the liaison with a growing rebellion against Arthur. The plot begins with Merlin's forebodings about Guinevere at the time of Arthur's marriage, and each poem adds something to the plot. Lynette challenges Gareth because she asked for Lancelot, the most famous of knights, but that fame is exposed as infamy through the words of a child; Geraint degrades his wife Enid as an object lesson for wives and later establishes a happy home away from Camelot as a testament against Guinevere; the brothers Balin and Balan accidentally kill each other because of Balin's disenchantment with Arthur's court—an extended effect of Lancelot's sin; the sacrificial death of Elaine; Lancelot's failure to find the Holy Grail because of his unworthiness; the beginning of the end of Arthur's reign, Vivien's 'rift within the lute'; the dramatic transformation of Pelleas into the wicked Red Knight shouting blasphemies to Arthur. The plot climaxes in "The Last Tournament" with Guinevere feeling from Arthur who, we are to believe, first learns of her infidelity from the Red Knight. The poem ends with the bitterness and fatal injury of Arthur.

In the *Idylls* Lancelot is acknowledged to be the greatest of the knights, but Tennyson uses his high station as a further indication of the seriousness of Lancelot's crime, insinuating that the low-born do not sin as seriously as those within the circle of the throne. Tennyson loses our support of his thesis when he tries to make Lancelot ignoble. At the beginning of the poem "Lancelot and Elaine", the knight is a guilty deceiver of the King, standing by Arthur's side and lying to him in response to a flirtatious look from Guinevere. The whole episode lacks dignity and validity as a few lines later that man who sins 'from such heights' unwittingly captures the heart of Elaine, the lily maid of Astolat, and the poetry describing Lancelot as first seen by Elaine is descriptive of a tragic hero, not a cheap roué. Tennyson refutes himself.

If Tennyson had written a new story or had he used lesser characters from the Arthurian legend we might accept the moral premise that he makes in the *Idylls*. No one challenges Tennyson's argument that adultery is a serious offense, nor that cuckolding a king is an offense with national implications. But Tennyson made a poor choice of villains; he chose to manipulate well-known and beloved characters to act out a tragedy that fails to move us. In the Arthurian tradition Lancelot is an epic hero, a famous warrior, father of Sir Galahad, purest of knights, and we refuse to look upon him as either foolish or evil.

Tennyson demeans both Lancelot and Guinevere to make them credible offenders. Lancelot's two-fold problem, "The great and guilty love he bare the

Queen/In battle with the love he bare his Lord" Tennyson solves by portraying a Guinevere who scorns Arthur as a 'moral child without the craft to rule'. Guinevere becomes a second Vivien, serpentine, contemptuous of her husband:

> "Arthur, my lord, Arthur, the faultless King,
> That passionate perfection, my good lord—
> But who can gaze upon the sun in heaven?
> He never spake a word of reproach to me,
> He never had a glimpse of mine untruth,
> He cares not for me. Only here today
> There gleamed a vague suspicion in his eyes;
> Some meddling rogue has temper'd with him—else
> Rapt in this fancy of his Table Round,
> And swearing men to vows impossible,
> To make them all like himself; but, friend, to me
> he is all fault who hath no fault at all
> For who loves me must have a touch of earth." (141)

If we must accept a Guinevere who ridicules Arthur, who neglects children, and who is libertine, then we must fault Arthur and Lancelot for the love they have for her. It would have to be a lesser man who would be content to select her as his queen, a far lesser man who would risk all to be with her. The fact is that the Arthurian legend has survived because Lancelot, Arthur, and Guinevere are characters of heroic proportions; and they are characters quite capable of memorable tragedy. Tennyson manipulates his characters to give credibility to his thesis, but because he narrows his characters to expand the offense, he defeats his own purpose.

Tennyson adds the story of Tristram and Isolt in "The Last Tournament", repeating the thesis of the negative effects of adultery and paralleling the tragedy of Lancelot and Guinevere. There are some significant differences in the story of the Irish queen and her illicit lover, as told by Tennyson, one of the most surprising of which is Tristram's role as spokesman for the theme of the poem! The legend of the second greatest knight has variations that make new interpretations of Tristram possible and believable, at least more so than with the characters in the central Arthurian story. In some versions, Isolt's husband, King Mark, is a kind man, in others, he is cruel; Tristram and Isolt fall in love because they both accidentally swallow a love potion, and in some versions the effect of the potion is life-long, in others it wears off. Tristram's marriage to a younger Isolt in Brittany and consequent return to his queen in Britain is optional. Tennyson uses much of the narrative of the Malory version, but Tennyson does not view his characters with the gentle permissiveness of charitable blindness that the soldier-writer of the fifteenth century did. Malory may be 'aristocratically sentimental' as Schofield says of him,[9] but Malory does deal with individuals, not heroes or anti-heroes; his readers are drawn into conversations between two people who love each other, two people whose honor and nobility are part of their tragedy:

> 'Then woll I nat be there,' seyde sir Trystram, 'but yf ye be there.'

> 'God defend,' seyde La Beall Isolde, 'for than I be spokyn of shame amonge al quenys and ladyes of astate; for ue that ar called one of the nobelyste knights of the worlde and a knight of the Roude Table, how may ye be myssed at that feste? For what shall be sayde of you amonge all knyghtes? "A! se how sir Trystram huntyth and hawkyth, and cowryth within a castell with hys lady, and forsakyth us. "Alas!" shall som sey, "hyt ys pyte that ever he was knight, or ever he shulde have the love of a lady." Also, what shall quenys and ladyes say of me? "Hyt ys pyte that I have my lyff, that I woulde hole so noble a knight as ye ar frome hys worship."'[10]

Tennyson has Tristram argue for free love in an exchange with Dagonet, the court jester, which in itself characterizes Tristram as somewhat foolish and frivolous. Dagonet provoked the argument because Tristram had won the rubies, symbol of innocence and purity, in "The Last Tournament", but did not award them to a pure maiden in the court, keeping them as a gift for Isolt. For this he is reprimanded by Lancelot, the women of the court; and the following morning openly insulted by Dagonet. Tristram degrades himself by listening to and arguing with one of Dagonet's station. The jester accuses Tristram of scandal against the court, and Tristram calls Dagonet a hypocrite, then sings to him the joys of free love.

Tennyson is never really awkward in his poetry, but he has made a poor choice of protagonist, and the traditional Tristram emerges in a lyrical passage that follows very quickly after the above scene. Thinking of Queen Isolt, he realizes that his marriage to the girl in Brittany was a mistake:

---

9. William Henry Schofield, *Chivalry in English Literature* (Boston: The Merrymount Press) p. 75.
10. Malory, pp. 506–507.

> But left her all as easily, and return'd
> The black-blue Irish hair and Irish eyes
> Had drawn him home. (216)

Suddenly Tennyson has reminded us of the gallant young knight who was fated to fall in love with another man's wife, a handsome young harpist who served Arthur well.

The issue of free love becomes the core of an argument between the now reunited Tristram and Isolt. This queen's description of the torments and ecstasies of her love for Tristram, her insistence on the magnitude and depth of the demands that love makes between two people is the only time in the poem that Tennyson discusses love as a powerful, personal experience; love is licentious or scandalous too often in the *Idylls of the King*; sin is its pervading personal experience. A debased king, an exiled queen, and a maddened knight were created by sin.

Tristram's argument for free love, "new life, new love, to suit the day" is lame, political. Again Tennyson is illogical, inconsistent: could Isolt really love a man who apostacizes as Tristram now does?

> The vows!
> O, ay—the wholesome madness of an hour
> They served their use, their time, for every knight
> Believed himself a greater than himself
> And every follower eyed him as a God;
> Till he, being lifted up beyond himself,
> Did mightier deeds than elsewise he had done,
> And so the realm was made. But then their vows—
> First mainly thro' that sullying of our Queen—
> Began to gall the knighthood, asking whence
> Had Arthur right to bind them to himself? (222)

We are not sure; is Tennyson's Tristram a mere propagandist or a tragic lover? The poem ends with the appearance of Mark:

> But, while he bow'd to kiss the jewell'd throat
> Out of the dark, just as the lips had touch'd
> Behind him rose a shadow and a shriek—
> "Mark's way," said Mark, and clove him thro' the brain. (224)

It should be obvious to the reader of this paper that the *Idylls of the King* were written by a great lyrical poet; the beauty and artistry of the poem are self-evident; the poem is a great artistic contribution to the continuing tradition of the Arthurian legend. And as a further gift to this tradition Tennyson created a new concept of Camelot—a place of infinite beauty and magic. He used his Camelot as a part of his plot, to enhance Arthur's spiritual significance. The characters in the *Idylls* are static, almost allegorical, like people in a fable. Tennyson does not attempt an interpretation of Lancelot's motives, rather, he pictures him as an intruder in a holy place; his is more the personification of the 'warring elements of the flesh' the more holy Arthur is; an Arthur in a sacred dwelling place deepens the dimension of Lancelot's sin.

The Round Table is the traditional center or core of the story of Arthur and his way of government; it was the meeting place for men of great physical and moral strength; knighthood, chivalry, and peaceful government radiated from the Round Table. Tennyson, however, uses Camelot as the focal point of all that is good and noble in the story. This Camelot adds a new dimension to the legend itself, an imaginative, creative dimension which the poet probably intended as a glorification of the throne of England—the monarchy, the reign of Victoria, an ideal state. His Camelot has become an ageless symbol, an ideal of an ideal, fairyland *and* heaven; a 'city of shadowy palaces…everywhere symbolic of the gradual growth of human beliefs and institutions, and of the spiritual development of man'[11]. The Camelot of the *Idylls* is the end of the rainbow; it is Tennyson's immortal tribute to the Victorian queen.

In "Gareth and Lynette" Camelot is a symbol, life's goal for the youngest son of Orkney, through whose eyes we see Camelot for the first time:.. 'The Lady of the Lake gateway—no gate like it in heaven; flowing with water, alive…and the city itself which 'moved so weirdly in the mist':

> a fairy king
> And fairy queens have built the city, son;
> They came from out a sacred mountain-cleft
> Toward the sunrise, each with harp in hand,
> And built it to the music of their harps. (33)

In the poem "Lancelot and Elaine", Camelot has some of the characteristics of the Christian heaven; it is no longer a development but the goal itself.

---

11. Tennyson, p. 442

Elaine, the lily maid of Astolat, tragically falls in love with Lancelot, dies and according to her own request, her body is placed on a flowery bier, placed in a boat and allowed to drift downstream to Camelot. Elaine describes her death wish to her father as a place beyond the 'shining flood'.. the home of the king...unable to visit it as a child she will go there in death. In this poem Camelot has overtones of an extended symbolism. Do we interpret Elaine's unrequited love for Lancelot as a symbol of human purity? Is she a martyr on the altar of love? earth's gift to heaven? The rain of diamonds over her bier from the hand of Guinevere, refusing Lancelot's gift, is overly dramatic, like a sacrificial offering. Arthur delegates Percival and Galahad, the two purest knights to bear her body into the large hall prior to a state funeral. It seems that in death, Elaine arrived.

We are troubled by this and other vague inconsistencies that occasionally surface in the poem. The last lines of "The Last Tournament" tells of Arthur's return to Camelot after killing the heretic Red Knight. Guinevere has fled to the convent, and Tennyson signals the end of Camelot:

> The great Queen's bower was dark—about his feet
> A voice clung sobbing till he question'd it,
> "What art thou?" and the voice about his feet
> Sent up an answer, sobbing, "I am thy fool,
> And I shall never make thee smile again." (224)

What was Guinevere's role in Camelot? What demands does heaven or the ideal state make upon a woman? How could one so unworthy as she who 'needs a touch of earth' be a part of an ultimate good or a present good? It must be more than 'Break not, O woman's heart, but endure'. Tennyson insinuates blame on Guinevere, but he never addresses himself to her problems.

Tennyson fails, also, to impress us with his King Arthur in the narrative passages of the poem. A king, or any great political leader must have the ability to rule; he is great because he knows how to use power. Tennyson fails to give us this King Arthur; he magnifies Lancelot's transgressions into a national scandal, but one man's adultery has never destroyed a nation; adultery's destructive power has always been in the realm of the individual, a private realm. Tennyson's failure to deal with this private realm deprives the poem of intellectual force and enervates Arthur and his queen. In the poem "Guinevere" the poetry is didactic and childish, almost offensively so with the poet using a postulant, young and detached from the world, to make moral judgments on a queen, and worse still, on a man and a woman in love. Her pious 'I pray for you both' is arrogant. The scene gets worse as the queen grovels on the floor as if in ecclesiastical humility, while Arthur reviews his great achievements, decides that she is not worthy to return to Camelot, and then god-like, forgives her. The scene increases in poetic fantasy as she 'perceived the waving of his hands that blest' and offered her:

> Perchance, and so thou purify thy soul
> And so, thou lean on our fair father Christ,
> Hereafter in that world where all are pure
> We two may meet before high God, and thou
> Wilt spring to me, and claim me thine, and know
> I am thine husband—not a smaller soul,
> Nor Lancelot, nor another. (238)

This sequence is illogical and symptomatic of the weakness of the whole of the *Idylls*. Tennyson relies too much on the device of using one character's weakness to accent the strength and purity of a character in apposition. If the kingdom fell because of the queen's weakness, then the kingdom was weak—Arthur was a weak ruler, and the premise of the poem is false.

Queen Guinevere proved to be too much for the poet; he stumbles because he fails to understand the ordinary problems that women deal with every day. It takes a skilled and sensitive writer to understand a woman's capacity to whore; he cannot regard women as subordinate men, but must recognize a woman's ability to spiritually destroy another woman by working through the weakness of a man. Tennyson's understanding of women is blatantly poor; otherwise, this paper would label the postulant in the convent and Elaine, the lily maid of Astolat, as the two worst bitches in English literature. And Tennyson had to go to Merlin, the wizard, for an empiric statement about women; Merlin is pompous, funny, as only men must learn that: 'For men at most differ as heaven and hell/But women, worst and best, as heaven and hell'. Tennyson's Guinevere is ill-conceived; she does not provide that hell; the two younger women could.

There are two inconsistencies in the Lancelot story that weaken the poem. Tennyson does not make it clear with whom Lancelot is at war, and the impact of the knight's erring ways is not convincing. The poet gives the impression that Lancelot is at war with God, but he is fuzzy on the limits of the earthly and the divine. If Lancelot is opposing a king, we do not believe that the example of one man could have the chain reaction that Arthur, the king, describes. Who was the leader of these men, Arthur or Lancelot? Did the strength of the Round

Table depend so much on one man's honor? If Lancelot is at war with God, then we sympathize with his humanity and look for god-like understanding from Arthur. The character Arthur has obligations as man or as God that are not met in the poem and because of this Tennyson fails to make Lancelot a serious offender.

The most important contribution the *Idylls of the King* makes to the Arthurian story is found in the isolated, fairyland areas of Tennyson's imagination. Away from reality, from the person-to-person dealings of everyday life, Tennyson is an attractive poet; he can take a moment, a single episode of life, a special place and add sights and sounds, emotions that we would miss on our own: Guinevere's tears in the convent are real, as is Lancelot's remorseful pain, and Arthur's "I love thee still. Let no man dream but that I love thee still." (237) And Tennyson's Camelot is a beautiful legacy to English literature; England itself is enriched with a new imaginative dimension.

The Idylls, however, present special problems to the twentieth century reader interested in a literary tradition. Any reader will agree that it is a charming poem for children, but the reader who looks for new insights about love or self-government, or a new intellectual appreciation of an old story will be disappointed. Tennyson's manipulation of characters is disturbing; the Victorian morality is intrusive; the thesis of the poem unconvincing; the story is weak. The problem may be that we expect a narrative only to find that the *Idylls* is really a static poem, that as Eliot says, 'for the narrative Tennyson had no gift at all...the outmoded attitudes toward relations of the sexes, exasperating views on the subjects of matrimony, celibacy and female education...we can swallow if we are given an exciting narrative'.[12]

The *Idylls of the King* fails to substitute the sin of Lancelot for the prophecy of *Excalibur*—an allotted span of life for Arthur. Tennyson's attempt to portray the 'dream of man coming into practical life and ruined by one sin' does not dominate the poem. He fails to make Lancelot the evil force he needs to be to effect change; his Lancelot is too introspective, his war too personal, too hidden. It takes an aggressive evil-doer, a Modred, to upset a kingdom.

---

12. T.S. Eliot, "In Memoriam" In *Tennyson's Poetry*, Ed. Robert W. Hill, Jr. (New York: W.W. Norton & Co., Inc.) p. 615.

SEPTEMBER 2003

In Retrospect,
   Tennyson chose a fool's errand in criminalizing Guinevere. We cherish our queens. We keep them precious in Literature and in our souls. Our Jackie Kennedy, Princess Diana, Evita Peron, Judy Garland and Whoopee Goldberg. Guinevere is queen forever.

BIBLIOGRAPHY

Barber, Richard, *King Arthur in Legend and History*. Ipswich: The Boydell Press, Ltd., 1974.

Eliot, T.S. "In Memoriam." In *Tennyson's Poetry*. Ed. Robert W. Hill, Jr. New York: W.W. Norton & Co, Inc., 1971.

Malory, Sir Thomas. *Works*. Ed. Eugene Vinaver. Oxford: Oxford University Press, 1971.

Schofield, William Henry. *Chivalry in English Literature*. Vol. II of *Harvard Studies in Comparative Literature*. Boston: The Merrymount Press, 1912.

Tennyson, Alfred Lord. *Idylls of the King and a Selection of Poems*. New York: New American Library, Inc., 1961.

Tennyson, Alfred Lord. *Idylls of the King*. Ed. Hallam, Lord Tennyson. New York: AMS Press, Inc., 1970.

0-595-31233-0

Printed in the United States
33174LVS00005B/325-327